CHASING FATE

Morayode

DISCLAIMER

This book is a work of fiction and true-life stories.
All true-life references to events, people, and locations are from the author's experiences and in no way establish any liability on the author from any parties whatsoever. Names of people, locations, and events, have been changed or modified to further exclude the author from such liabilities.

DEDICATION

For: Dan, Michelle, Peter, Justin, Daniel, and the little
ones not yet here.

CHAPTER ONE

The sun was already setting as Nadia trudged along the boulevard. It was seven o' clock, but the neighborhood kids were still out on the street, playing or sitting around swapping stories as they stalled or ignored their mothers' calls to come in for the evening meal. A group of adults was gathered outside Mr. Okafor's house obviously taking advantage of the cool evening breeze, a remnant of the good weather from the Atlantic Ocean. Mumbled replies welcomed her as she greeted them; Mr. Okafor was also in their midst, and he smiled proudly as he broke a kola nut and crunched half in his mouth.

Nadia shrugged, finding it strange but unable to delve into adult business at the moment. Strange, because on Tuesdays Mr. Okafor would already be at work at the National Electric Company on the other side of town where he worked into the early hours of the morning. He would also be driving into the boulevard as they left for school on Wednesday morning, honking his horn and nodding as they greeted him. Strange, also, because he had certainly gotten friendlier these past few months, as if he had won the lottery.

There were many guesses in the neighborhood as to why: his wife had just opened a bigger store at the local market selling provisions and other household wares; he'd finally gotten the supervisory position he sought so earnestly at the electric company; the community association just recently made him treasurer; and his oldest son, Anthony, graduated from university with honors in the United States and was coming back home to Nigeria for some quality family time before returning to commence his master's program in engineering. All these were theories, but nobody knew the truth behind his most recent happiness.

Nadia ran into two of her friends, Chioma, and Ngozi, both playing marbles on the sidewalk.

"Nadia, do you know your father is at home?" said Chioma. She was fifteen years old but wise beyond her years.

The kids knew Mr. Yakub, Nadia's father, very well, and for good reason. When he came walking down the street, they dispersed like spilled water, dodging into their own homes and any nook and corner they could find. Mr. Yakub was a no-nonsense man, and he disciplined everybody's kids like his own whether the parents liked it or not.

He favored an authoritarian parenting style and demanded that all the females in his household cover their hair at all times. Despite modernism, a lot of Muslim households in Nigeria still required headscarves to be worn by their women. Of course, Nadia and her sisters wanted to be fashionable like other females their age and had resorted to all kinds of ways to be like their contemporaries without incurring their father's wrath.

They would cover their hair before leaving the house, take the scarf off after a couple of yards, go about their business, and put it back on a few yards from the house when coming back.

"Are you sure?" Nadia asked the two girls.

"Yes, Nadia," Ngozi, the most talkative of the lot, answered as Nadia draped a brown floral scarf over her head.

"Thanks. See you later," Nadia said, picking up her pace.

She was tired, hungry, and eager to eat dinner. She was so engrossed with trying to secure the scarf that she failed to notice three males walking in her direction. Suddenly, she found herself smacking against a hard body.

"Oh, sorry!" she apologized immediately as she looked up into the face of her victim.

He was almost a good head and a half taller than her. He steadied her with his hands and would not let go immediately. She could not help noticing how handsome he was. His square jaw was masculine yet tempered by lips that were parted in clear surprise as his clear brown eyes investigated hers, as if trying to decipher a mystery by looking into her very soul. She could discern a tiny scar just above his right brow, and the little gap between his two front teeth only added to his sex appeal. For a moment, they seemed lost in time, lost in each other's gaze, until his two male companions coughed in amusement.

She came down to earth at once, pulling back. "I am so sorry!"

"It's OK. It's OK." His hands were strong yet gentle on her arms as they steadied her. She tingled from the contact as alien warmth suffused her body.

She stepped back suddenly as if burned. He was easily six feet tall, and his very white teeth was a sharp contrast to his ebony black skin. His hair was in a low box cut, and she could see the vein in his neck as if magnified. Even her senses were heightened. He had on a white T-shirt, and his jeans were a dark blue rinse color. A simple gold necklace complimented his casual look. The evening breeze wafted his cologne into her nostrils. It was masculine, musky, and it smelled wonderful. She breathed in sharply, confused, and alarmed.

He watched her with narrowed eyes, taking in her appearance in one sweeping motion, and extended one of his strong hands that had burned her earlier, but she refused.

"Are you all right?" his voice was deep, gentle, and genuinely concerned.

"Yes. Yes, I am. Bye." She glanced briefly at his friends' still amused faces and walked briskly away from them. Soft laughter followed her, but she didn't dare look back, afraid she would run back into his arms just to experience that warm feeling once more.

Dinner was in progress when she got home. Her mother was busy with the soup, and the youngest wife, Rashida, was pounding yam in the mortar with all her might. It wasn't an easy task to make pounded yam for a big family of fifteen: her father, three wives, and twelve children in total. But she had signed up for it, marrying into a household as big as Mr. Yakub's, who was proud of having three wives. Nadia's mother, Basrat, was the first wife with five children. Nadia was also the family's firstborn. She had four siblings: Jaleel, Rakhya, Hadeed, and Zayed. The second wife, Reeskat, had four children: Ahmed, Khaeera, Alee, and Rasheed. At twenty-five, Rashida the youngest wife was barely older than Nadia herself. Her children, Miriam and Suleman, were the youngest children in the house.

As Nadia went about her chores that evening, her mind was unsettled. All she could think about was the man she had bumped into earlier. Her body warmed up whenever she remembered his touch, and she prayed silently for God to forgive her for thinking such dirty thoughts, especially about a man she barely knew. Certainly, she had never met anyone like him. He didn't look like he belonged around here.

After much wondering, she concluded that he had to be the one and only Anthony Mr. Okafor had been doting on. He certainly looked like a decent guy, but, sigh, she couldn't afford to think about him, or any other guy, for that matter. Her father was extremely strict, even as he warned his daughters whenever he lectured them after morning prayers for them not to marry outside the household religion. Well, that took care of Anthony right there because Mr. Okafor and his family were staunch Catholics. Secondly, she still had to graduate from high school, whereas Anthony was on his way to a master's degree in another country. Thirdly, there were so many "worldly" girls in Festac Town, he wouldn't even give her the time of day. She doubted if their paths would ever cross again.

At that point in time, the only thing Nadia wanted to do was finish school, pass her post-secondary exams, and get admission to study medicine at the University of Ife or the University of Lagos. She couldn't wait to get out of secondary school and begin college life because she was actually older than most of her classmates, who turned eighteen after they graduated. The family had moved around a lot in her younger years because her father worked for Siemens and transferred every year or so to another state in the country.

He always would move all the family with him, believing staunchly that families need to be always together if a coherent household is desired especially with as a large household as his. However, these moves sometimes came with consequences, and Nadia was held a class back from her real grade when she was thirteen.

She was troubled though because her father had been so adamant that she enroll in a correspondence writing course from the Writing School of England. Nadia started writing children's stories purely as a hobby and for her friends' entertainment at the age of nine. Her father had taken interest and encouraged her, but she didn't want to make a career out of writing.

She had grand ideas about making a difference in the world and believed being a doctor would create a pathway for her to do that. Time would tell.

As soon as the evening prayers were over, she ate dinner, took a bath, and retreated to the backyard of the bungalow to enjoy a late night breeze before bed.

"Nadia, have you seen Anthony?" her younger sister, Rakhya, said excitedly as she joined her on the bench, her eyes wide with excitement. "Oh, he is sooo handsome!"

"Hmm…" Nadia raised a brow. Rakhya could be dramatic at times.

"Really? That is all you can say? Oh my God, he was walking the streets today with his friends, and all the girls were just gushing over him. He answered when we said hi and waved to us. Do you know that he bought his dad a new car? And Nkechi said he brought so many goodies back from the US. I am going over to their house tomorrow!"

"Why?" Nadia asked, unwilling to disclose that she had indeed met him or that he had any effect on her, too. "You and Nkechi don't really like each other."

Nkechi was Anthony's younger sister, aged fifteen, attended the same school with them but acted like she was better because she went to a private school; Nadia couldn't stand her at all.

"Well, today at school I decided to make up with her, and she invited a couple of us to her house tomorrow. I just want to catch a glimpse of Anthony. He is sooo fine!"

Nadia sighed and shook her head. Rakhya was the outgoing one, always hanging out with friends. Though they had two years between them she suspected that her sister was already dabbling in things she had no business doing, just because of the company she kept. She loved going to the picture studios and had been in several fights even, most of which their father was not aware of because their mother was always covering for her.

Nadia knew she did not have time for kissing ass just to see Anthony. Nothing pleased Nadia more than curling up with a good book and reading into the wee hours of the morning, sometimes even forgetting her chores. Her friends were few but close, and she spent time with them also, but the last thing she would do was run the streets or start seeking out some guy because he just came back from the US.

"All right, Rakhya, have fun but don't come crying when you find out he has a girlfriend. What makes you think he'd even look at you? You're just sixteen!"

"Hmm…age doesn't matter." Rakhya smiled, swished her skirt, and stuck out her tongue. "You're just jealous because I am going to their house tomorrow, and you're not."

Nadia sighed again, shaking her head, and smiling as she watched her sister go. "These little girls…"

In the quiet and solitude, Nadia's mind wandered, wishing she were just a child again without a care in the world. She looked forward to life after high school but was still scared of the unknown.

From a faraway place in her subconscious, she divvied up random memories from her childhood. One incident stood out, and she laughed at herself as she remembered bygone days of innocence.

Next day after dinner, Rakhya gushed about going to Anthony's place, how nice he was, how wonderful his family was, all the goodies they got from him (chocolate bars, candies, and T-shirts), and how she couldn't wait for him to ask her out. Nadia listened to her with semi-interest, eager to know yet afraid to show that Anthony had gotten under her skin. She had spent the whole day at school daydreaming about him. She just couldn't get that charming smile off her mind, and the tingling sensation of his touch still lingered. Every time she thought of him, goosebumps rose on her arms. It was a scary yet delicious feeling.

"Are you not going to see him?" Rakhya asked.

"Why should I?"

She shrugged. "So, you can get chocolate and a T-shirt, and you can give them to me if you don't want them."

Nadia laughed. "I trust you, Rakhya. Ever the opportunist."

"You know me. I like to mingle," Rakhya replied. "Anyway, they're having a party for Anthony on Saturday, and we have been invited. It's going to be a big party to celebrate his graduation."

"I am not going."

"Suit yourself." Rakhya said. "I already know what I'm going to wear. My purple and gold gown, and I'll borrow one of mom's necklaces."

"What about your hair? You'll probably be the only girl at the party with her head covered."

"I don't care. I already told Mom, and she's buying me a gold shawl tomorrow. It will match nicely with my dress, and I'll walk like a princess, like Cinderella…" Her voice tapered off dreamily.

Nadia sighed in exasperation. She left her sister dreaming about Anthony and went to bed.

Sleep did not come easy that night. Saturday was only three days away. She so much wanted to catch a glimpse of Anthony once again, though everything in her common sense told her that was not a good idea. She had never been the slightest bit interested in the boys around her because none fascinated her enough to engage her in thoughtful conversation. She loved intelligent men especially when they combined it with wit and humor. She wanted a Prince Charming like the ones she read about in the romance novels she swapped with her friends.

And she also wanted a career for herself. She loved her family but felt her mother and stepmothers could do more for themselves if they were more educated. None of them worked outside the home, and Nadia believed her father took advantage of that. Her father was a nice man but sometimes he wasn't nice to his wives at all. Nadia didn't blame him, though. The wives bickered too much over little things, and it was enough to drive even her crazy at times. Nadia wanted more than this mundane yet chaotic existence. She wanted an intelligent, funny, handsome, Prince Charming who would come in from nowhere and whisk her away on his powerful horse into the sunset. Dreams.

Nadia loved to learn and usually stayed after school to study because the house was always full of raucous children running around. Fridays, she liked the most because only a few people were on the school grounds, and the principal let them stay until six pm. She had her favorite place to study, and there she was after school, engrossed in logarithms when she heard her name called softly.

"Nadia." That voice. She looked up, surprised to find Anthony standing over her desk. He was looking even more handsome than she remembered. He was wearing a short-sleeved shirt, light blue, worn over dark blue jean shorts with brown loafers. The gold chain was still around his neck, and he was alone. And she couldn't take her eyes off his legs. They were strong and solid, and if he hadn't been a man, she would have thought them beautiful. "Hi."

Nadia was apprehensive not because he was there, and they were alone but because she didn't trust herself around him.

She gulped as words tried escaping her mouth. "How...?"

He smiled as he grabbed a chair and sat beside her. "I believe we are yet to be properly introduced. I know you're Nadia, and I'm Anthony."

He extended his hand, and this time, she did not resist. She welcomed the warmth because it was so beautiful what she felt as they shook hands. She wondered if he felt it too because he kept her hand in his for a minute.

"What are you doing?" he asked.

"Studying, as you can see," she replied. "I like the quiet. And what are you doing here, by the way? Last I heard, you already graduated from college. You certainly don't need to be mingling with us high schoolers anymore." She felt more confident as she found her voice. "And the security guard wouldn't like it if he found you here."

"I know. I was wondering, isn't it dangerous, you being here all alone by yourself?" He looked around. "There's hardly anybody in the compound, and the security guard is outside the gates."

Nadia shrugged. "I know I'm safe here. It's a school for God's sake, and there are usually a lot of us, but because it's Friday a lot of students went home early." She got up and packed her books. "And it would be a good idea if I did the same."

"Please don't leave because of me." Anthony stopped her. "I didn't mean to bother you. I just wanted us to talk. That's all."

Her eyes narrowed suspiciously. "Talk about what? If you think I'm one of those girls, you must be"

"Geez, calm down. I don't think anything. I just want to be friends!" he exclaimed. "Why are you so defensive anyway? Your sister is friendlier. She came to the house the other day, and she's all open and easygoing."

"Then go talk to my sister!" Nadia replied, infuriated. "In case you've forgotten, you invited yourself into my domain."

He laughed. "Such big words! Nadia, I just want to talk to you, OK?" His voice softened. "Let's be friends?"

"What's the point? You'll be going back to the US soon anyway," she stressed, looking into his eyes. And at that moment, she could see herself in them. She had zero dating experience, but she had never seen the tenderness in Anthony's eyes before. "I'm too young for you!" she snapped, bringing herself back to the present. "And we're from totally different backgrounds."

"Wow! Wow!" Anthony's laugh was loaded with warmth. "What are you talking about Nadia? It hasn't come to that yet, OK? Can we sit down and talk for a minute? I like you a lot, OK? I want us to be friends."

She shook her head in futility. "I don't know what it is with you wanting to be friends. How can we be friends when you're only here temporarily?" She reluctantly sat back down. "It's almost six, and I need to be getting home before evening prayers start."

"Where's your scarf?"

"My scarf? You don't expect me to wear a scarf to go to school, do you? Even my father knows better. Policy is policy. His freedom stops where the school gates begin. The school only allows uniform caps on campus."

"You are a spitfire of words, aren't you?" he said amusedly. "I like you a lot. I've heard a lot about you—"

Her eyes narrowed in suspicion. "From whom?" Nadia was a very private person, but no amount of privacy could hide everybody's dirty linen; it was part of the fabric that wove the boulevard together.

"Don't worry, I have my sources. Are you coming to the party tomorrow?"

"No."

"Why?"

"'Cos, I don't want to, don't see the need to, and I have a math exam on Monday, I have to study very hard for over the weekend, so I don't flunk. I'm having problems with graphing equations, and it's driving me crazy. This new teacher Mr. Phillips 'supposedly' studied in the United States, and he says he doesn't want to spoon-feed us, but God, he's making things worse. He starts explaining and then goes, blah, blah, blah." She stopped talking when she noticed the look on his face. "What's funny?"

"You, going on and on about Mr. Phillips. I can help you; you know."

"Hmmm…"

"I'm an engineering major, in case you haven't heard." He raised his brows in pride. "A little bit of math won't kill me, especially if I have to tutor a student like you."

Her eyes lit up. "Really?"

"Why not? We can meet up tomorrow, and I'll teach you an easy way to solve graphing equations. Two to three hours should be enough."

"But tomorrow is your party. You'll be too busy."

"Trust me, if I had a choice, I wouldn't attend the party myself, but I have to make the old man happy, you know. Besides, the women are taking care of all the preparations. All I need to do is show up. If you want, we could meet up here at ten in the morning and be done by twelve, but only if you will attend the party."

"So, there's a catch." She tapped her fingers on the desk. "You know, I'm showing up at the party 'appropriately dressed,' right?"

"So? You are beautiful with or without the scarf Nadia." His eyes swept her up and down. "Come naked if you want to. I won't mind."

She couldn't believe her ears. "What?"

"Just teasing. God, you're something else. I won't pounce on you in the midst of everybody you know. Come on, let me walk you home."

"You're certainly fearless because I know you've probably heard of my dad, and you don't care." She adjusted the straps of her messenger bag, glancing at him from the corner of her eye. "You don't care, do you?"

He shrugged. "I respect my elders, as long as they respect themselves. I'll walk you some distance, and you do the rest yourself."

They fell into step easily, side by side, greeting the security guard on their way out the school gates. "Why are you doing all this? I am sure you have a hoard of girls clamoring for your attention."

"You wouldn't believe, Nadia. Sometimes I have to turn off my phone just so I can have so quiet time. Nigerian girls can be very persistent even in the face of rejection. It's ridiculous, some people I do not know from Adam or Eve ask if I remember the time we went on breaks together or walked back from school together or sang in the school play together."

"That's the nature of human beings, you know. You are incredibly attractive, successful, and smart. Of course, people would want to be around you. Just accommodate as you can and let go gently. It's a small world, even if you live in the USA."

"Wise girl." He touched her arm gently, sending that tingling sensation down her body again. "I like you a lot. Do you like me?"

"No!"

"Liar!"

They were almost at the beginning of their street. Nadia's house was among the first row of houses while Anthony's was further down. The boulevard was comprised of three-bedroom bungalows side-by-side on either side of the street, and children were still playing outside. A few of them stopped to wave at Anthony as they walked by. He had become a kind of celebrity because he came from the US.

"Is this OK?" he enquired as they neared her house. "So, we meet tomorrow at ten, where?"

"At the primary school, a few blocks away from my school. I'll be in the very first classroom near the entrance."

"You'll be there?"

"Sure, I really need a good score to boost my math grade."

"All right." He stood looking at her for a moment, not caring about the prying eyes of neighbors who saw them together. "Later."

"Bye," Nadia's smile was wide as she watched him walk ahead of her.

"Nadia!" said Chioma. "What are you doing with Anthony? Wow, girl, you are fast. I thought you weren't into guys"

Nadia sighed. The girl had a way of materializing from nowhere. "God can't a girl catch a break around here? we're just friends Chioma. That's all. Before you start blabbing to everybody."

"I'm not a blabber!" Chioma retorted hotly. "I just like disseminating information."

Nadia shrugged. She knew better! "All right keep this information to yourself, though I know that it's impossible. We're just friends, really. Where's Ngozi?"

"Gone to the market with her mom. So, what were you two talking about?"

Nadia pretended not to know. "Me and who?"

"Why you and Anthony, of course. I have two eyes, you know."

"Hmm…," Nadia said. "Are you sure it's only two eyes 'cos you see everything. Nothing is going on,"

"If you say so." Chioma walked with her almost to the entrance of her house. "All right, are you coming to the party tomorrow?"

"Why is everybody talking about this party? Yes, I'll try." Nadia said bye to Chioma.

Nadia's father was outside on a chair. "Good evening, Daddy." She could feel a tension in the air as he watched her narrowly. She touched her head, just to make sure her scarf was there.

"Nadia, what are you doing with that boy?" he grated.

His question stopped her in her tracks. "That's Mr. Okafor's son who just came back from the US, Dad. He was just introducing himself to me."

"Remember, they are not Muslims," her father stressed.

"Yes, Daddy," Nadia said quietly.

That was all her father cared about. Not that she was too young to even be having any kind of conversation with Anthony or any other man in the first place. Not about Anthony's character as a person and a man, but only about Anthony's religious denomination. Sometimes, she believed her father would let one of his daughters marry the devil himself if he converted to Islam!

Her father used to be a very loving dad. Even though he was not the affectionate type, he used to let them know how much he valued education and would love to see them all go to college. Sometimes after morning prayers, he would lecture the family, stressing the fact that even though he had a lot of children, he wanted to show society that having lots of children does not mean one couldn't take proper care of his family. However, things changed when he joined an Islamic sect that did things a bit different from the usual daily prayers. He was stricter on the children especially and leaned more toward the more traditional way of doing things. Nadia was apprehensive of her future after high school.

Anthony was already waiting when she got to the study location on Saturday morning. He was sitting on a step watching cars pass by.

"You look so normal," she commented. "One wouldn't think you just came from the US. Maybe by the way you talk, but you blend in nicely."

"Really?' He flashed her a smile, looking at her all over. "You look nice."

"Thank you."

Nadia had taken her time getting dressed that morning, leaving her mother wondering as she watched her in askance. Nadia was never one for frivolities. Her mother had seemed skeptical when she told her she was going to the primary school to study for an exam. She had chosen a flowing floral gown in red, white, gold, and blue, and adorned her head with a matching blue scarf. Her father was against his daughters painting their fingernails, but her feet were well pedicured and thrust into white sandals. Though she didn't like wearing too much jewelry, she loved earrings and had them in every color one could imagine. To complement her dress, she had on blue dangling bangles to match the head tie.

"I hope you are a good teacher." They walked into one of the classrooms, and she brought out her study guide. "At least better than Mr. Phillips."

"Why don't you guys tell him you don't like his method of teaching?"

"Tsk, tsk! He would never listen. He says that is how math is taught in the US. Anyways, all I need to do is get an eighty on this exam, and I'm good. I can't wait to be out of his class. I thought I was doing pretty decently in math until he showed up and turned everything upside down!"

For the next hour and a half, Nadia listened attentively as Anthony instructed her on the simplest ways to solve graphing equations, and she steadily began to grasp the concept. He was indeed a good teacher. He was patient with her, willing to explain the same problem five times if he had to until he was sure she understood what he was trying to do.

Around eleven-thirty, he suggested they take a break. "All work and no play…" He closed the study guide and turned to her abruptly. "Tell me about yourself."

"Nothing much to tell really. I am sure your sources have told you everything."

"Just on the surface, and there are no 'sources.' What are your dreams, your ambitions? Do you want to travel someday, marry, have kids, what are your career goals?"

"Anthony, I'm just eighteen, barely out of high school. What career goals? Right now, I just want to be able to pass the JAMB and get admission into a good university…" Her voice trailed off softly.

The Joint Admission and Matriculation Board exam, similar to the American SAT, was a make or break for every student. Students could be the smartest and still score ridiculously low. Nadia didn't know how the Board scored the tests, but without it one couldn't get admission to any public university in the country. People graduated and sometimes waited two years to get into college just because they couldn't pass the JAMB exam. To her, the system needed a better standard of tests. Until then though, every high school graduate was at the mercy of the almighty JAMB.

"Will your father let you go to college?" he asked pointedly. "I've heard quite a bit about him, too. He certainly has his ideas about this religion thing."

"I don't know. I don't really want to think about it."

"You could come to the US."

"How?" She looked at him as if he were crazy. "I would never get a visa. Eighteen, unattached female with no responsibility in the world."

"Well, I'm going to promise you one thing, Nadia, right now. Anytime you make it over there, I will take care of you until you get settled, OK? That's a promise."

Nadia didn't doubt him for a minute. In Nigeria, everybody in the neighborhood was like a brother or sister, and it wasn't uncommon for people not totally related to engage in acts of kindness like they were.

"I'm not a pessimist, so I will take you up on that offer. What time is it?"

"Quarter till twelve."

"We need to be going. My mom says she wants me to run some errands for her when I get back."

"Sit down, Nadia." He pulled her down as she started to push the chair back. "We'll leave soon, OK?"

"Why do you have so much interest in me? I mean, you are going back the US soon, aren't you?"

"I don't know. There's just something about you…I can't put a finger on it myself. You are so fresh, so intelligent, you say what's on your mind, and you don't pretend."

"Pretention is stupid. Just be you and people can either take it or leave it."

"There you go. That's my Nadia."

"I'm your Nadia?" She fought to hold back her laughter. "Is that how it happens in the US? Have you even asked me if I wanted to be your Nadia?"

She was joking of course, but Anthony took it seriously. He moved closer to her and took her hand in his and looked deeply into her eyes. "Do you want to be my Nadia?"

"Even if I agreed, it would be foolish of me because the distance is too great. How do we go on dates? On a fighter jet every other week back and forth between wherever you live and Lagos?"

"Why can't you just answer with a yes or no?" He seemed frustrated, all of a sudden.

"Anthony, you're twenty-three, and I'm eighteen, OK."

"OK. I'll come back next year and marry you."

It was her turn to laugh. She threw back her head in amazement. "Are you serious?"

It wasn't uncommon for families to arrange marriages for their sons living in diaspora but the Okafors and Yakubs were not that close. Unless, of course, if Anthony insisted. And even if so, religion would kill the vibe. Mr. Yakub would never allow his daughter to marry a Christian because that was automatic conversion to the Christianity. Life was so unfair sometimes.

"Yes, Nadia, I am serious. Why do you find that funny?"

She didn't have an answer for that. Even if she did, he wouldn't like it. "We really must get going."

"Yes." This time, he didn't stop her. "So now you must keep your end of the bargain and come to the party this evening."

"All right. A bargain is a bargain."

They fell in step naturally again, as if they were meant to be, but he turned her toward him suddenly and planted a light kiss on her mouth before she could stop him and hugged her tightly afterward. Electric shocks reverberated through her slim body as she came in contact with his hard frame. But she loved it and wanted it. Her arms went around his waist as she laid her head on his chest.

"Thank you," his voice said above her head.

"For what?"

"For a nice time, even though we were studying." He planted a kiss on her forehead. "Let's go before Mr. Yakub starts raising hell."

"My father is not that bad," she protested. "He has a big household to run, and he must devise whatever means necessary to keep his household together."

"I reserve my comments." He smiled at her as they walked back home.

CHAPTER TWO

It was well past eight at night when Nadia showed up at the party. The Okafors' home was packed, and so was their front yard. Chairs had been set up outside for guests, and a big party tent gave some privacy and protection from the weather. She recognized a lot of people from the street, including a few friends from school and Rakhya hanging out with her friends in a group away from the adults. Nadia greeted a few of the neighbors, including Mr. Okafor at the entrance of the house before finding a seat in the living room. That was where the young adults were enjoying themselves drinking, eating, and playing pop music.

Anthony was nowhere to be found. His two friends from the other day recognized and waved to her, which unnerved and surprised her at the same time. When a guy's friends take the time to be friendly, he must have told them something. She hoped he didn't tell them that Nadia was "his girl."

Some of Mr. Okafor's extended family members were present also, including Aunt Edna, who Nadia knew because she was a frequent visitor to the house. Kate, Anthony's younger sister, twenty-one, was there too and gave Nadia a derisive look as they crossed paths. Kate had graduated from Festac Grammar School and was in her second year studying economics at Lagos State University.

Nadia was a very tolerant person, but she couldn't stand Kate at all. The girl thought she was a princess and should be worshipped by her "clique." Well, Nadia didn't have problems with any girl thinking she was a princess, but the worship part, she didn't get at all. In high school, Kate was part of a clique who behaved as if they weren't home trained, and sometimes bullied other students. Nadia had even chosen her as a mentor, and she declined the offer on the pretense she was already mentoring three people. But Nadia knew that was a lie because she accepted Nadia's best friend, Grace, who was so excited to be the only "school daughter" and suggested Nadia make a go for it so it would be two of them.

A school mother-daughter relationship was like having a school mom, usually a grade or more higher, and who looked out for the school daughter as a real mother would. She might buy gifts for the school daughter, mentor her, give her pocket money, or even prevent her from being bullied. In return, the school daughter would run little errands for the school mom, and all this took place on the school grounds. After that last bell rang, everybody went their separate homes. Some school mom-daughter relationships lasted for years; however, if the relationship was strong enough for both students to stay attached even beyond high school years. Nadia would have been excited to have Kate as a school mom, but she wasn't surprised she had declined either. She considered her a snob, anyway. As the environmental monitor, Kate had also unfairly called Nadia out many times without cause to pick up trash left by other students, which Nadia didn't find funny at all. It puzzled her greatly because she couldn't figure out why Kate disliked her so much. For one, there were a good four years between them, and they weren't even in the same grade.

Bottle of 7Up in hand, she sat quietly in a corner and observed all the fun going on, glad that she was there anyway, even if it was under obligation. People were certainly having fun. Nadia was wearing a short-sleeved maxi dress made from the traditional Ankara fabric popular among the Yorubas from the western part of Nigeria with a matching scarf and ballet flats. For jewelry, she picked medium-sized silver bangles, and her makeup was sparse: foundation, eye pencil, and lip gloss. Mr. Yakub would never let anyone put on lipstick in his house, even his wives.

"Care for a dance?" asked one of Anthony's friends, Lanre.

Nadia was surprised as well as flustered. "Er…"

"Come on," he dragged her onto the dance floor as Pitbull and Ne-Yo's "Time of Our Lives" started playing.

"I'm not a good dancer—" she started protesting, but he placed her firmly in front of him.

"Just move, Nadia. Girl, have some fun!" He laughed as he gyrated to the upbeat music.

It was awkward at first, but Nadia soon found herself moving in tune with Lanre's antics on the dance floor. He was really comical as he danced and made funny faces at her. Nadia laughed unreservedly, unaware that somebody else was watching them from the doorway.

The number soon ended and Usher's "You Got It Bad" came on, but she declined to dance again and slowly made her way through the throng to her seat.

"I'm having this dance," said Anthony from behind her.

She turned, almost gasping in surprise at how handsome he looked in his designer short-sleeved shirt and skinny jeans.

"Of course, you know I can't dance with you," she whispered under her breath. "It's a slow song!"

"All the more reason." He pulled her toward him while still maintaining a safe distance. "I don't want word getting back to Mr. Yakub about me doing dirty dancing with you," he joked.

Nadia couldn't keep her eyes off him as they danced, yet she noticed the imaginary daggers from other females in the room as they stared at her. She soon got into the groove of things and even moved closer to him, letting him hold her hands. She liked contact with Anthony because it made her feel really nice. Her body tingled whenever in contact with his, and she was afraid her knees would turn to Jell-O right there.

"You look really nice, Nadia,"

"Thanks. Might I say you're mighty fine yourself, Mr. America."

He shook his head in futility. "You're a case, aren't you? Mr. America, haha. Come here." He stopped dancing and pulled her arm. "I want to show you something."

"Anthony."

"Sh!" he chided as he propelled her toward the backyard, the only place not teeming with people. Anthony currently had full use of the boys' quarter for the duration of his stay in Nigeria, and he had furnished it to his taste, a blend of traditional and contemporary pieces, free of clutter. Nadia stood in the middle of the living room while Anthony proceeded to the mini bar.

"I don't think this is a good idea, Anthony."

"Why are you protesting, Nadia? Give yourself some room to breathe. You want something to drink? Or we can go back to the party if you want."

"No, I've had my fill of soda for the day." Being here alone with him was making her nervous. "Anthony—"

He suddenly strode toward her and stopped her with his lips, kissing her gently as he pulled her into his arms. His lips were firm yet tender. He released her slowly, reluctantly. "I wish I could take you back to the US with me."

Slightly shaken, she sat on the big plush sofa in the living room, breathing heavily. He sat beside her and pulled her into his arms again. "I'm just gonna hold you, all right?"

She sighed in defeat as she nestled into his arms, her ears picking up the rhythmic movement of his heart as it beat strongly against his chest. She reveled in the masculine scent of his cologne, feeling secure and protected as she had never felt in all of her eighteen years. Both knew there was no need to talk, it was just enough to be with each other like this and bask in the moment.

All kinds of thoughts raced through Nadia's mind. This could not be love. She knew because love didn't just happen in two days with a guy she just met four days ago. Even with all the romance novels she had read, she really didn't believe in love at first sight. Infatuation perhaps, but not love. Anthony might be fascinated by her now, but as soon as he went back to the US, she would be history. Even at twenty-three, he still had a lot of life ahead of him, and the odds were greatly stacked against them from all angles anyway. The whole situation was even surreal to her, and the more reason she should tread carefully. Her body tensed, a consequence of her thoughts.

"You all right?" he asked with concern. "You're awfully quiet."

"Yes."

Just then, a figure entered the room. It was Aunt Edna. She took one look at them, eyeing Nadia contemptuously as she scampered out of Anthony's arms.

"Anthony, your father's been looking all over for you."

"Yes, Auntie," Anthony was in no hurry to get up. Casually he made for the door with Nadia treading carefully behind him, afraid to even look Auntie Edna in the face, but she was promptly stopped.

"Nadia, I need to talk to you for a minute."

Anthony wanted to wait for her by the door, but she ordered him to go see his father, Nadia would be following momentarily.

"What do you think you're doing with my nephew?" she asked once Anthony was out of earshot.

"Nothing, Aunt Edna. We're just friends."

"Well," she looked Nadia up and down insolently. "You looked more than just friends from what I saw when I came in here. You need to stay away from my nephew because you are not his type. Do you know that he has an American wife?"

"No."

"And you both don't belong together. Stay with your kind, Nadia, and I don't want to see you here while Anthony is around."

"I only came because Anthony invited me to the party, Aunt Edna!"

"Then let this be your last visit while he's around. Anthony has a bright future ahead of him, so don't go and complicate things. Do you hear me?"

"Yes."

"So, we're good. You can go."

Furious and upset that there was only so much she could say without being rude, Nadia stormed out of the boys' quarters.

Outside, Anthony was being toasted by his father in a gathering, and Rakhya was nowhere to be found. It was almost eleven thirty, and the party seemed to have grown bigger as the night went on.

Seething with anger, Nadia walked back home with the resolve not to ever see Anthony again. Mr. Okafor was a decent man but the behavior of the females in his household left much to be desired. Anthony's mom was OK, but one would not want to mess with her when she was in one of her moods. Nadia didn't get it at all. They all lived in the same neighborhood, for Christ's sake.

Monday was uneventful at school. Nadia managed to get an eighty-five on the math exam. She really wished she could thank Anthony in person. Despite the incident at the Okafors that marred her weekend somewhat, she was in good spirits as she made her way home from school, walking with Grace. Even as they conversed, Nadia was absentminded. She had been so excited to share her feelings for Anthony with Grace but not after that encounter with Aunt Edna.

"I heard you and Anthony danced at the party." Grace was close to her and probably knew more about her than any other person.

"What about it?"

"Is it true you're his girlfriend?"

"Nothing of the sort. Where do you people get your information?" Nadia played it cool. "We just had a dance like everybody else."

"But he chose you," Grace hassled. "Why don't you just come out and say it? Nadia, you've been too quiet." They were almost at the beginning of the boulevard, where they usually parted ways. They spied Anthony slightly leaning against a car. Nadia pretended not to see him.

"Hi, Anthony!" Grace beamed, waving.

"Nadia," he called, but she just kept on walking, trying not to notice how handsome he looked. "Nadia, I need to talk to you."

"What is up with you, Nadia?" Grace asked puzzled, jerking her arm.

"I don't want to talk to him, OK?" Nadia picked up her pace. "You should be on your way home, Grace."

Adamant, Grace followed her at a good pace until she finally relented. "OK. See you tomorrow then."

For the next several days, Nadia went through the motions of her life like a robot. She missed Anthony terribly but knew it was best to leave him be. Despite the pull she felt in her heart she knew a relationship with him was unrealistic and futile. Besides, if she was feeling this way while he was still around how would she feel when he finally went back to the US?

She caught snippets of information from Rakhya, who was an Anthony fan anyway, as to what was going on over at the Okafors. Anthony repainted the house. Anthony took his friends to Badagry Beach for a picnic. Anthony this, Anthony that. It was enough to drive Nadia nuts, but she was determined to not see him again.

Three weeks later, Rakhya appeared with an envelope addressed to Nadia. It was from Anthony. He had gone back to the United States but left his number and address in case. Against her better judgment, she filed the letter away while pondering what to do with it. Their encounter, though brief, had awakened something in her that was beautiful and frightening at the same time. Certainly, she knew what to expect when with a man she liked: tingling sensations, feelings of security and warmth, and the ability to be herself. Now more than ever, she yearned to be independent and explore the world.

Most people passed the JAMB in two sittings, and Nadia was no exception. Except for her, it was a path that deviated totally from her plans to have a career in medicine. Her father saw her not making the JAMB score as an opportunity to dissuade her from going to college. He started hinting that it might be a good idea for her to attend journalism school and getting a two-year diploma, dashing her hopes of going to college totally. He tried to convince her to stick to writing since she was good at it anyway, which Nadia didn't understand. Journalism and medicine are on contrasting sides of the spectrum with no relation whatsoever. She pointed out that she could still write while still being a doctor, but his mind was made up. She pleaded with him and even solicited the help of neighbors and family to change his mind, but to no avail.

She spent the few months after the failed JAMB in a sort of mini-vacation phase with her friends. They went to the beach, even a few parties, and she watched as one after the other some of them left for college. She was hopeful and even started studying for the next JAMB, but before she knew it, he had paid for the two-year diploma course and she found herself watching in helplessness as her peers all went off to college while she stayed at home.

To make matters worse, he enrolled her in a six-month secretarial school in Festac Town, so she could hone her "typing" skills, while she waited for her first semester at journalism school to commence. She did very well at the secretarial school and was more than happy to be on her way out the door.

Nadia's misery in journalism school was short-lived. She figured that she might as well make the best of it since knowledge gained is knowledge for life. Some of her lecturers where actually news anchors and reporters she had seen on the local TV station. The instructors were inspiring, and she started seeing this phase of her life as a stepping-stone to her life ambition. She could make connections, and connections could lead to fame, fortune, and privileges not bequeathed on ordinary humans who were not in the journalism circle. It was powerful and heady stuff, and it fueled her desire for greatness even more.

For an internship, Nadia was sent to the *Daily Time*s office at Ikeja, where she was paired with a nondescript roving reporter called Momoh. Momoh was a handsome young man, but he didn't make an effort when it came to his appearance. His shirts were sometimes not ironed, he seemed to wear the same pants every day, and throughout their time together he only wore two pairs of shoes, the second pair only after the first one got so worn out, she suggested that it might be a good idea for him to get another pair of durable shoes. He didn't care what anybody thought about him, but he was a darned good journalist and managed to get scoops that others could not, which suited the editor fine.

Momoh helped polish Nadia's story-writing skills. Before long, Nadia was getting her own bylines in the newspaper, sometimes alone and sometimes with him. She felt immensely proud seeing her name in print attached to a story.

Soon, though, the internship was over, and then came the hard part: getting a full-time job. Luckily for her, she had made some friends at the *Daily Times* and soon approached several smaller newspapers under the *Times* umbrella about writing for them. Before long, she was regularly contributing stories to the *Sporting Record* and *Lagos Weekend* and earning some money albeit not enough to sustain much.

Writing for the *Sporting Record* meant she had to be at the National Stadium in Surulere, where she mingled with other reporters and met sports dignitaries from Nigeria and all over the world.

Nadia yearned for more. After paying for journalism school, her father somehow thought he was done with his duties to her as a father and stopped giving her any money. The money from her freelance stints was meager, and she constantly had to say no to men who thought they could get her into their beds with their empty promises.

She was barely out of journalism school when her father took on a new agenda, marrying her off. She didn't understand the logic behind this latest obsession, and she fought vehemently against it. He brought all kinds of men to the house, and even though she would have dated some of them under different circumstances, the mere thought that she was not free to choose a man for herself left her repulsed and determined never to marry any man recommended by her father. It was galling and a very low point in her life.

She found solace by reading, cooking, and spending time at Grace's house. She also started hanging out with other journalist friends at the National Stadium, which proved to be very rewarding as she was actually able to meet celebrity athletes and important sports figures in Nigeria. Even at twenty, Nadia was very skinny and often mistaken for much younger, and this was an added advantage for her because people gravitated to "the young woman who seemed to actually know what she wants and is striving toward it."

One day, the Secretary of the Boxing Federation told a few of the reporters about an upcoming fight in Las Vegas between two world heavyweight boxing champions and gave everyone interested in going a form to fill out with their respective employers. As a freelancer, Nadia was on her own, but on a whim, she obtained a form and took it to the *Sporting Record* editor. He was hesitant at first but asked if she had an international passport. He warned that she might be disappointed because the embassy wasn't giving visas to young adults especially if they were unmarried but went ahead and filled out the form anyway. Nadia couldn't contain her excitement, but she celebrated reasonably under the circumstances.

The only person she told was Grace, who was in her second year studying information engineering at Lagos State University. The day of the interview at the American embassy met her with more uncertainties and doubts than she had ever had in her life. Nervous, she walked slowly to the interview room with a silent prayer under her breath. The consular officer was, however, very friendly.

He looked over her passport. "Why do you want to go to the US?"

"To represent the *Sporting Record* in the upcoming fight." Her hands were tightly wrung in her lap.

He fixed his eyes on her for some minutes. "OK. Come back tomorrow for your visa. Good luck." He shook her hand. Nadia couldn't believe it. She hadn't even spent ten minutes in the interview room. It felt like a dream as she tendered her passport and walked out of the huge gates. She really was going to get a visa! Her editor couldn't believe it, either.

He beamed with pride like a new father. "Wow, you are one lucky girl, Nadia. Do you know how many people have tried and never gotten a visa? God is really on your side." He bade her sit and gave her some fatherly advice for about an hour. "Be careful when you get there. Not everyone you see is your friend even if they pretend to be. I hear some Nigerians dabble in things they are not supposed to, so make sure to stay away from trouble. I know you can make it. You're a very smart girl. And don't forget to write, OK?"

She picked up her visa before telling Grace the good news. Her friend was, of course, happy for her, but wondered how they would come up with the money for the ticket.

"What are you going to do Nadia?"

"I don't know, Grace. I know Mr. Okafor loans money to people sometimes. Maybe he'll loan me the money, and I can pay him back." It was common knowledge that Mr. Okafor loaned money to people in the neighborhood because he had easy access to American dollars, which was going for a nice exchange rate against the Nigerian naira.

"You know that's not possible. Your families are not that close, and I don't think he'd loan any twenty-year-old that much money, either."

"Yes. What was I thinking? They would think I'm going to meet Anthony, and I don't know anybody, either. I actually don't want too many people to know about this really."

Nadia had no option but to tell her father about the visa. He seemed really surprised but then praised that her good luck was because he had sent her to journalism school. If she was in college, would she be making the necessary connections to get a visa? He was happy for her and promised to help her get a loan from his bank, which she could pay back once she got to the US. That settled the matter of the ticket, but she still had no place to stay. She didn't want to call Anthony even though he had promised her she wouldn't have any problem getting accommodation if she came to the US.

She set out two months later for the United States on British Airways with a stopover in Amsterdam.

She felt free for the first time in her life and had a blast in Las Vegas, but the Nevada event soon passed, and Nadia was almost stranded once accommodations ran out. A lot of her journalist friends went back home, but she still had several months left on her visa and wanted to explore the United States in any way she could before she even thought of going back to her mundane journalist life and authoritarian father in Nigeria. In the end, Grace referred her to a friend who lived in Pennsylvania with her fiancé. With money running out, she used her last cash to buy a Greyhound ticket.

Florence and her fiancé, Ben, met Nadia at the station. Florence was a curvy lady in her mid-thirties, full of life, and always optimistic. Ben was a bit more reserved but friendly, nonetheless.

Nadia had a room all to herself in their apartment on Mellon Street. It was a quaint little neighborhood, and sometimes on the weekends, they went to watch the Green Bay Packers while they trained at a nearby stadium. Florence and Ben were nature lovers, and they took Nadia on long walks with them at local parks in the evening.

Florence asked Nadia several times if she was planning to stay in the United States instead of going back to Nigeria and was skeptical when Nadia told her about Anthony. Nadia tried calling Anthony's number several times but kept getting his voicemail. She left messages twice and stopped calling him, thinking he probably couldn't care less anyway. Besides, she didn't want to start trouble since Aunt Edna had told her that he had an American wife. Florence and Ben reiterated it was best not to call, citing numerous incidents when people living in the US had promised those in Nigeria they would help them get on their feet, only to betray and ditch them at the last minute.

Nadia soon found her way around. Her favorite places to go were the laundromat and the library. The laundromat was primarily to wash clothes, but someone had set up a shelf with lots of books to while away the time, and she took advantage of that.

Florence and Ben started weighing her options if she stayed and figured she could start get a head start as a foreign student, although the process was complicated and expensive. In between, they had a busy social life and would usually visit friends on the weekend. Nadia couldn't have been happier. These people did not know her, and they took her in and treated her like a sister. Life was good.

Then Anthony called, saying that he had been traveling and just came back to her messages on his phone, and for her to come down to Houston.

Florence and Ben tried to dissuade her from going to Texas "because you can't really trust anybody."

"But he's not like that. His family lives on the same street as mine. What harm could he possibly do?" Nadia tried to justify her decision. "Besides, I can't keep feeding off you guys forever."

"But we don't mind. Once you get an ID and a job, you'll start finding your way, including going to school."

Nadia debated within herself for a week, then bid farewell to the nice couple and got on the Greyhound to Texas. It was a two-day journey, but she enjoyed the scenery and the beauty along the way, especially in Texas. Such a big state with endless roads, and she couldn't wait to see Anthony again.

He met her in Downtown Houston at six in the evening, casually dressed in slacks and shirt with loafers. He was just as handsome as she remembered. She hugged him briefly and awkwardly because she hadn't taken a shower since leaving Pennsylvania.

Morayode

"How have you been?" he asked on the ride home. "I'm so sorry I didn't get back to you on time. I was traveling, job-related duties. I called immediately when I got your messages. You're looking good." He smiled. "What happened to your head tie?"

His mirth was infectious. "You know better, Anthony. So how have you been? Your wife?"

"Wife?"

"What about your American wife? I surmise you wouldn't have invited me if she didn't approve, right? For me to stay with you guys even for a while?"

"I'm divorced, Nadia. She didn't take too well to having family around and picked little fights with my mom. It was either a divorce or a life of being miserable. I loved her very much, but I just couldn't take it anymore."

"I hear the culture is different."

"Definitely, this is an individualistic culture. The family can come around for short visits and holidays but not stay indefinitely like back home unless that's the agreement. Not to say there are no exceptions, but…" He shrugged. "She was very unreasonable. You must be very tired."

"Yes."

Anthony had a two-bedroom condominium on Meadowglen along Gessner Road. After Nadia showered, he took her to McDonald's and got her burgers and fries.

They sat talking in the living room well into the night. He made no attempt to touch her, and she didn't demand any affection. There was really no relationship even with the feelings from two years ago, and she wasn't sure if he still felt the same way. Time had passed.

They went to separate rooms around twelve midnight. Nadia lay dreaming, feeling a little bit secure since she first landed in the US. She was confident that Anthony would take good care of her, no matter what. With this thought and a smile, she fell asleep. The next day, she woke up early. He was already downstairs making a bagel for himself, smartly dressed in brown slacks and tan shirt with cufflinks.

"Good morning."

"Morning, Nadia." He smiled at her affectionately. "What would you like for breakfast? Bagels, bread? Anything you want is in the fridge."

"Work?"

"Yes, we'll talk when I come back, OK? Do not open the door for anybody whatsoever. I'll call to check on you. There are a couple of magazines by the fireplace, and a few books on the shelf. I know you like to read. And you can watch TV, too. Here's the remote." He showed her how to work the channels and volume. "See you later, OK?"

"OK. Have a nice day."

"Lock the door behind you." He grabbed his briefcase and left.

The condominium was a fair size for a two-bedroom. The living room was downstairs, with a guest bathroom, and the two bedrooms upstairs each with its own bathroom. Nadia explored with caution, not wanting to invade Anthony's privacy.

After breakfast, toast with eggs and bacon, she grabbed a copy of *People* and plopped on the huge couch and became fascinated with the antics on the *Jerry Springer Show*. Is a mother sleeping with her daughter's boyfriend? Is a married man cheating on his wife with her sister? She couldn't believe it. How could people expose themselves on national TV like that? After the *Jerry Springer Show*, *the Bill Cunningham* show came on, then *the Maury Show*. She was so engrossed that it was one o'clock before she felt hunger pangs. She craved some real African food like pounded yam and spinach soup but made do with a BLT sandwich instead. The pots and pans were all packed away, and it didn't look as if a female ever lived there.

Nadia missed home, especially her best friend, Grace. The last time she talked to any member of her family was the previous week. Even though she felt relaxed in Anthony's place, her future was still uncertain. How did she go about getting a work permit? Looking for a job, making new friends, and blending in with her new culture? She watched TV, read, fell asleep, and read some more, and was dozing off when she heard the bell ring. Anthony was home. Excitedly, she opened the door for him, throwing herself at him in a hug.

"So glad to see you!"

"How's your day? Hope you weren't too bored." His voice was cool, distant.

"It wasn't that bad, and I made myself a sandwich for lunch. There's nothing to eat around here!" She followed him into the living room. "Don't you eat African food?"

"I'm a bachelor. What do you expect?" He laid his briefcase on the dining table and looked her deadpan in the face "I found you roommates."

Nadia stopped in the middle of admiring his nicely dressed frame and stared at him, nonplussed. "What?"

"I found you roommates."

"I thought I'd be staying with you until I start finding my way around here…" Her voice trailed off. Was this the same Anthony who had promised to take care of her when she came to the US? If he had no intention of doing that, why had he invited her from Pennsylvania all the way to Houston? "You promised me."

He was unwavering. His voice was not cold, but it did not have the characteristic tenderness with which he talked to her. "Lizzy is a nice girl. Very street smart but nice. She lives on the other side of town."

"Why?"

"I'm sorry, Nadia, but you can't stay with me. I'll take you there tomorrow morning. You are young, and I don't think it's a good idea for you to be here living with me."

"So why did you invite me here, Anthony? I thought we had a connection in Nigeria. You promised to help me if I ever came to the United States. So, what's changed?"

"Let's not go into details, Nadia. You'll be all right."

"But I don't have any money. How am I going to pay rent? I had thought you would help me to get working papers and all. Florence and her fiancé were going to enroll me as an international student at a nearby community college close to their house."

"I'll pay the first month's rent for you. I'm sure you'll find a job soon and make new friends and find your way from there."

Nadia couldn't even muster the energy to argue with him. "OK."

She shrugged and went up to her room to start packing all the clothes she'd unpacked the night before. She couldn't fathom what had gone wrong between the time he left for work with "We'll talk when I get back" to his coming back and telling her he found some roommates for her, somebody without a common tie whatsoever. She relied on her friendship with Grace to trust Florence and Ben and on the proximity of their families to trust Anthony. How was she going to trust a girl named Lizzy who she didn't know anything about other than her street smarts and blunt proclamations? If this was going to be the pattern of things to come, then she would better off remembering all the advice from her editor.

One crucial thing, he said, was for her to obtain a green card to legitimize her stay in the US and make it easier to get grants to go to school. She wouldn't be able to vote for a while, but it was a step up from being illegal.

She refused to go down to eat dinner. Her anger was palpable, and she took a shower and went to bed. She didn't want to face Anthony at all because doing that would cause irreparable damage to their relationship. Her anger was that deep. She thought they made a real connection when he visited Nigeria. He was not even married right now, and her staying here would have been a great opportunity to reconnect, but he obviously did not feel the same way anymore.

47 | P a g e

CHAPTER THREE

It was a silent and painful ride to Lizzy's apartment the next day. Apart from a stilted "good morning" to Anthony, Nadia did not see the need for small talk about what had transpired the previous night. She was not even angry at him because she was an independent woman and never really relied on anybody for much anyway.

He cast a quick glance at her as he pulled into the parking lot of a small apartment complex on Beechnut Street. "Are you all right?"

"I'm fine," she replied, looking around. Most of the buildings were two-storied with lots of trees in front. She spotted the laundry room just to the right of a three-storied Five Hundred Building. Nadia couldn't help but appreciate Anthony's ease of grace as he retrieved her one piece of luggage from the trunk of his Jeep Cherokee. Their eyes locked but none of them said a word.

Lizzy was nothing like Nadia imagined, but she was certainly a spitfire of words and rambunctiousness as she ushered them into the one-bedroom apartment. Anthony promptly introduced them, declined to be hosted, and handed over half of the month's rent.

As soon as he left, Lizzy explained that there was one other girl living in the place, Bukky, who worked second shift at Jack in the Box and had an American boyfriend, Andre. There was only one bed in the place, and there were no chairs in the living room. Nadia would have to buy a mattress or airbed to sleep on. Lizzy soon found a used mattress off of Craigslist, which she lay on the living room floor to sleep. Sometimes however, Nadia slept on the bed when Lizzy was working night shift at her job. The apartment did, however, have a tiny balcony where the girls gathered and exchanged gossip in the evenings.

"So how did you know Anthony?" Lizzy asked.

"Our families are neighbors in Lagos," she replied. "And I was in Pennsylvania before he called me out of the blue and asked me to come down to Houston."

Lizzy shook her head in amazement. "So why did he ask you down here if he has no intention of helping you out? You know he only paid half of this month's rent. How are you going to cope? Do you have any money? Can you even work?"

Nadia explained her predicament but explained that she was ready to start making her way and taking care of herself. By the end of the day, she determined that Lizzy was indeed a nice woman although very outspoken to a fault sometimes. Nadia actually thought that Lizzy tried too hard to present a "tough girl" image so people wouldn't take advantage of her.

Later, Bukky came home, and Nadia didn't know what to think of her. She was obnoxious and had tall tales of how she was very popular at the Nigerian Television Authority premises, even though she didn't work there. Nadia wasn't that a much of a prude to decipher what she was actually doing there, probably dating some of the big wigs, but she kept her thoughts to herself.

Bukky also took her into the kitchen and showed her where her things were kept with an implicit warning on how she didn't like people messing with her food. Lizzy was amused by Bukky's territorial attitude although Nadia didn't find it funny at all.

It was nice for a while. Nadia walked around the complex a lot during the day and got to know some of the neighbors including Barry, a Ghanaian who lived right opposite them and attended the University of Houston and worked part-time to support himself. It was obvious to everybody that Barry had a crush on Lizzy, but he might as well have had a crush on the Rock of Gibraltar because Lizzy couldn't have cared less. They, however, got together sometimes at his place to watch movies when he was off from work.

Nadia's roommates were very active on the social scene. They attended a lot of parties, but Nadia always declined, which infuriated Lizzy.

"You have such a pretty face, Nadia. Why don't you go with us and have some fun? Don't you get tired of being in this house by yourself?"

"I got things to do, Liz," Nadia would reply. "I need to get going, get a job, get legalized, something. I've been here two months and I owe you rent."

"Call Anthony to help you out."

"No!" Nadia retorted hotly.

"Does he ever call to check on you?"

"He called last week," Nadia said dismissively. "Do you think I can't find my way without him?"

Lizzy let it go, but Nadia was miserable because Bukky wasn't helping matters at all. Nadia had never encountered that kind of person in her life. Bukky thought about nobody but herself, and they had gotten into fights twice because of her attitude. Nadia didn't even remember what the first fight had been about, but the second one was about a pot of soup Bukky kept in the fridge.

She had come home from work one day in a bad mood, gone to the fridge to get some food, and complained that a piece of chicken was missing from her soup. Nadia couldn't believe her ears. They were still going back and forth on the missing piece of chicken until Lizzy laid matters to rest by saying that she was the one who ate it the previous night because she was really hungry and there was no other food in the house. Nadia already distrusted Bukky, but that incident sealed any negative opinion she ever had of the rude girl. She steered clear of her completely after that even though they lived in the same apartment. She didn't need to worry though because Bukky and Andre were soon engaged, and she began spending more time at his place.

Well into the third month, Lizzy came home one evening very excited. "Nadia, I got you a job!"

"Really?"

"Yes, at Mimi's Restaurant as a waitress."

Nadia had heard a lot about the restaurant, a popular hangout for Nigerians since several of them owned businesses along that strip of road in Houston.

Nadia couldn't sleep that night. Anything was better than nothing. They both went to see the owner the next day. Ms. Mimi was a jovial woman in her mid-forties with a gold tooth, which she got when she visited Mecca for the Hajj pilgrimage.

She had a daughter who was also named Mimi, a spoiled seventeen-year-old who treated the cash register like an ATM machine. She was the only child, so her mother accommodated a lot of impetuous behavior, especially the way Mimi behaved with the male customers, some of whom she followed home sometimes. Nadia watched, but it was none of her business. She was more concerned with guarding the cash register because Mimi had the expensive habit of taking taxis to the restaurant and rummaging through the register to pay for the fares. Sometimes, the poor drivers would be outside for upward of ten minutes especially when the register had just been emptied before she made her grand entrance.

Nadia liked the job. The pay was only $7.50 hour, but as time went on, she was making a lot of money from tips. The customers liked her, and it was not uncommon for her to even out the day with forty dollars in tips. One time, a customer who had been wanting to go out with her wrote his phone number on a hundred-dollar bill. Nadia thought it was a joke, but he laughed and told her to keep the money.

Life couldn't be sweeter, but Nadia wanted more. She started paying her own share of the rent, buying a few things for herself, and even scrimped enough to send some money home to her family by hiding it in a greeting card.

Nadia also started finding out what men were really like. She was smart enough to know what they really wanted from her, although a few serious ones refused to give up, promising her heaven and earth. Juliet, the other waitress at the restaurant, didn't understand her at all. She was present when John, a Corvette-driving regular, asked Nadia asked out on a date, which she refused.

"You're crazy!"

"Whatever! I don't know what he does for a living, hanging out here with his friends all the time. The other day, he said he would give me a credit card which I could go to the mall and spend however I liked. Can you believe that?"

Juliet was nonplussed. "Let me guess. You told him no?"

"Of course, I did!" Nadia replied, walking away as Juliet shook her head perplexed.

"Crazy girl!"

She made some good friends, including Bayo, who worked for a jewelry company and had a Ghanaian girlfriend named Mavis, who was suspicious of Nadia from the get-go when they were introduced at a July Fourth barbecue event at Bayo's condominium. In the beginning, Bayo was very nice to her. He often gave her rides and invited her along to parties with his friends, but he soon started giving her the cold shoulder. He had been teaching her how to drive, and Nadia just asked him what was wrong.

"It's you," he replied.

"What have I done? All you need to do is tell me so I can correct any wrong, Bayo. Why are you being cold to me?"

He didn't even look at her as he drove her back home. "My friends think I'm stupid."

"What? What has that got to do with me?"

"They think I'm stupid because of you. Here I am giving you rides, taking you out, and helping you out with money sometimes, and you're not giving me some!"

"Oh my God, is that what this is about?"

"Yes, my services are not for free!"

"But you have a girlfriend!"

"So? Look, I can't help you anymore if you won't put out, OK? I may be nice, but I am not stupid."

"OK then."

And that was the last time she ever saw Bayo again. Nadia knew she should have known better than to think the driving lessons were actually free. She was learning a lot from being in the U.S., especially the saying that "Nothing is free." Lizzy warned her about this.

Fearful that the incident would repeat itself with other men who offered her rides, she started taking cab rides to and from work with

Lizzy pitching in whenever she could. The restaurant was only ten minutes from the house by car and double that walking, but she couldn't walk because she got off at eleven in the night. With time, she was able to make friends with two cab drivers who knew her schedule and helped her get home when notified on time.

A lot of bachelors frequented Mimi's Restaurant, and Nadia wasn't surprised when Anthony came in one day with a friend. By then, Nadia had put on a bit of weight and looked different from when she first arrived in the United States. She had filled out nicely, and sometimes patrons couldn't even tell she was African unless she talked.

She served Anthony's table herself, and she couldn't help but notice the way he was looking at her. Before he left, he promised to call her the next day.

He didn't call the next day, but he did call four days later, apologizing for taking so long and asking if she could come by his place for a visit.

Her alert radar went up at the invitation. "I don't know if that's a good idea."

"Come on, Nadia. I see Lizzy and your other roommate at parties all the time, but you're never with them. You don't work every day, do you?"

"OK. I'm off on Saturday. You can pick me up."

"Good. I'll see you then."

Nadia told Lizzy about Anthony's invitation.

"I really don't trust anybody anymore," she stated.

"Anthony is harmless, as far as I'm concerned. Maybe he feels guilty for what he did to you and wants to make things right."

"Too late for that now, but I'll go anyway, just to get out of the house."

Lizzy laughed. "That, certainly, I totally agree with."

Nadia spent time on her appearance on Saturday. Her hair was swept up in a ponytail, accentuating her oval face and nicely angled cheeks. She borrowed one of Lizzy's outfits, a little red dress that flared just below her waist and stopped just above her knees. Of course, her love of earrings still waxed strong, choosing a pair of silver nuggets with matching bangles. She had splurged on a pair of nice platform shoes the previous week while shopping at the mall, and she slipped into them, smiling as she examined herself in front of the cheval mirror.

"Nadia, girl, you look so nice. You really should go out more often!" Lizzy exclaimed on seeing her. "Wow, you look really good. Your face is so pretty."

"Please, Lizzy, don't start."

"You know me. I call it as I see it. You are one hot mama!" Lizzy laughed. "Hold on." She adjusted the zipper of the dress in the back. "Looking good!"

"Thanks! Oh, he's here!" Nadia could hear knocks on the door. It was Anthony, neatly dressed in casual shorts and a tan polo shirt.

He was smiling, just like she remembered from back in Nigeria. He stared at her appreciatively. "You ready to go?"

"Yes, let me grab my bag."

He exchanged pleasantries with Lizzy, and he led Nadia downstairs to his car. He was now driving a Ford Explorer.

"You bought a new car."

"Yes, the Jeep was due for trade-in. Once I start spending a certain amount of time and money on a car, it's time to get rid of it." He was gentleman enough to open the car door for her, making sure she was comfortably seated before going to the driver's seat. "Do you want to grab something to eat?"

They drove to Taco Bell and ordered some chicken chalupas and lemonade.

Nadia was glad to be with him but cautious as to his true intentions. "How's your family back home?"

"They're good. All doing well. Kate graduated and now works for a bank on Victoria Island. Nkechi is retaking her second JAMB exam, and my mom opened a second store. My dad is well, still at NEC, looking forward to retirement. He can't wait to pay me a visit. How about your family? Your dad and siblings?"

"They're good. I talk to them regularly, and my father still asks me if I still pray five times a day."

The sound of his laughter made her smile also. "Mr. Yakub will never change!"

"You got that right!" Nadia said.

They soon pulled up to his condominium. There wasn't much change from when Nadia visited last. She kept her emotions in check as he got out of the car and came round to open the door for her. A lump rose in her throat as she remembered the way he calmly told her he found her a roommate. She watched as he opened the front door, noticing his nicely trimmed fingers. Anthony took good care of himself.

"Nothing has changed at all," she observed as they walked in, and she made herself comfortable on the sofa.

"I'm usually working anyway, and I have a lady who comes in to clean twice a month." He sat beside her. His eyes were appreciative of her simple yet elegant outfit. "You look so different."

"How?"

He turned to face her. "Much more beautiful than I remembered. You seem to be doing really well."

She shrugged. "I guess. I am not doing badly at the restaurant. Nigerian men are very generous with tips, I realize, so I might as well give the best possible service to get as much as I can."

"Don't they ever ask you out?"

She gave him a mischievous look as she unwrapped a chalupa. "What do you think?" she extended one to him. "You want?"

"No, I'm OK at the moment. Don't try to evade the question."

"I wasn't trying to." Nadia took a healthy bite. "Of course, they ask me out. And I say no."

"You've never met somebody you like?"

"No…hmm…I love chicken chalupas."

"You haven't changed a bit. Always be yourself no matter what. That's what I love most about you. You're so authentic."

"Really?" She raised her brows, letting bygones be bygones for now. "How do you define that?"

He stared her straight in the eye. "Fresh, honest, knows what she wants, ambitious, warm, caring, considerate—"

"OK, OK! I get it, I get it!" She laughed. "Please don't make me choke on my food."

She quickly grabbed her lemonade and took a long sip. She could feel tension in the room: raw, unapologetic, sexual tension. She looked away, suddenly steeling herself against his charm.

He finally ate one of the chalupas and they sat in companionable silence for a while. Nadia didn't protest when he nestled her into his arms as they watched TV well into the night. She dozed off, only to be awakened around midnight with her head still on his chest.

"Bedtime."

"What time is it?"

"Twelve. Come on." He led her upstairs but steered her toward his room.

"Anthony…"

"Shh!" he interjected.

"I don't think—"

"It's OK, Nadia, I'll just hold you, OK?"

"Anthony, I actually don't think this is a good idea. I mean, what is the purpose of spending the night in your bed?"

"Nadia, don't jump to conclusions, OK? I have missed you. I just want a fresh start. We can talk, OK?"

Against her better judgment, she gave in to his persuasion. Nadia wasn't that naïve to not know that anything could happen, but she realized that her feelings for Anthony would always be there. He handed her one of his T-shirts to wear, which she thought was enough cover up before getting into the huge bed in the middle of the room. Anthony wore only pajama pants, but she wasn't alarmed. She tensed up when he pulled her into his arms, but soon relaxed as they talked. About everything but them. Nadia was afraid to bring up a conversation that hinted at any kind of relationship because she didn't know how he felt. Maybe this was just a booty call for him. And if it was, well, she surmised, she would take it as that because she needed it, too.

He held her all right, but sometime in the night, nature took its course, and she was helpless against the passion his touch evoked in her. She had wanted him ever since she first laid eyes on him in Nigeria, and he proved to be a caring and considerate lover as he gently guided her with passion until both of their desires were fulfilled.

He held her tightly afterward. "Why didn't you tell me you've never—"

She stopped him "It's OK. I don't regret anything, I wanted it, too."

"Oh, Nadia, come here." He kissed her deeply. "I love you. I've loved you since you bumped into me four years ago."

"Really?" Nadia couldn't believe Anthony was telling her he loved her, but it might just be that he was caught up in the moment. If he loved her, wouldn't he have wanted her to stay with him when she came to Houston on his invitation?

He could see the skepticism in her eyes. "Just like that. That is one thing with us men. We just know when we meet the one." He kissed her gently on the forehead. "Go to sleep, love."

They spent the entire weekend together. Nadia was a changed woman when she went back home on Sunday night, and Lizzy noticed it immediately.

"Wow, girl, you need to go out more often, specifically to Anthony's," she joked.

Nadia rolled her eyes. "Oh, be quiet, Liz!"

But the teasing wouldn't stop for a whole week. Anthony called on Monday night, then on Wednesday night, but then she didn't hear from him for a couple days and called him on Friday. He didn't pick up the call. He didn't call back. She tried repeatedly for the next week, and eventually her calls just went straight to voicemail.

Thinking that he probably was on one of his business trips, she didn't make a big deal about it.

A month went by. She could feel Lizzy bursting to ask questions on why she hadn't been going to Anthony's place, but she was reluctant to jump to conclusions or talk about the issue.

It was a busy Saturday at Mimi's Restaurant. The usual closing time was eleven at night, but Nadia didn't get to take off her apron till midnight. Exhausted, Nadia didn't protest when Mimi the daughter suggested a ride. She too had worked a bit that night, and even Nadia was surprised at the way she handled the customers. The girl could really be nice and hardworking when she felt like it.

Dealing with mom and daughter at work was not bad, but Lizzy was getting the itch for more already. She couldn't definitely wait to get a better job soon enough.

"I really appreciate it, Mimi." She smiled when they entered her complex. "And you did really well tonight, too."

"You're welcome, Nadia. See you tomorrow."

"Bye,"

The lights were on in the apartment, which was unusual because Bukky was supposed to be spending the night at Andre's, and Lizzy had taken on a second job as a caregiver at a senior living facility, working nights including a double shift from Saturday night until Sunday at ten in the morning. Hesitant, Nadia put her key in the lock, only to have it open and reveal Lizzy standing there with an odd look on her face.

Nadia sidestepped her into the apartment. "Aren't you supposed to be at work?"

"Yes. I was very hungry and came home to grab something to eat. I wasn't in the mood for fast food. And I wanted to tell you something."

"What is it?"

"Anthony is married."

"Really?" Nadia asked calmly. Somehow, she knew it was true. "How do you know?"

"My friend Angela told me when I bumped into her at Walgreen's today. That's why he hasn't been picking up your calls. He's been in Nigeria all this while for his traditional wedding and just came back three days ago with his wife. He actually threw a little party for a few close friends last night, Angela included."

"Oh my God," Nadia sank into the used couch they had pooled money to buy on Craigslist. "Oh my God, oh my God!" She covered her face with her hands. "No!"

"Nadia, quit it. You knew yourself there was no future with Anthony. His family would never let him marry somebody, not from his tribe. You knew, didn't you? Personally, I think he just used you girl. Men!"

"But he told me he loved me, Liz. How could he do this to me? He invited me to Houston on the pretense that he would help me then kicked me out of his house after just a day, he abandoned me without caring how I would survive, dumped me on you—"

"You weren't dumped on me, Nadia!" Lizzy said, coming to sit beside her. "You more than pull your share of weight in this apartment, and you are a very good roommate."

"But it's true, Liz, however you look at it. I mean, why did he invite me to his apartment as if he really cared, tell me he loves me, and then abandon me again? The worst thing is, I knew it could just be a booty call, but I didn't care because I love him."

Lizzy rubbed her on the back empathetically. "Just forget about him, Nadia. You're doing good for yourself. Once you get a better job and start school, you won't think about Anthony again. I always thought he was sneaky. For him to do this to you…well, you know men."

"But I am pregnant, Liz." Nadia dropped the bombshell she had been concealing for the past couple of days. "I have been pregnant for four weeks and didn't know it until I went to see a doctor two days ago. What am I going to do?"

"Oh my God, Nadia. How could you not know?"

"Because I saw my period last month, that's why. Except for the current cycle, which was two weeks overdue. That's why I went to see the doctor, and he recommended a pregnancy test just in case."

"Wow…I don't know what to say, Nadia. What are you going to do now?"

"I'm still thinking about it."

"You're thinking about it? You can't keep this baby!" Lizzy exclaimed, looking at her watch. "I've got to go back to work. Don't do anything rash OK. We'll talk about it some more. Even this is too much for me." Lizzy sighed as she left. "Take care. I'll see you later."

Despite Lizzy's protests, Nadia decided to keep the baby. It was by no means an easy decision, but she had no choice. She also swore Lizzy to silence on the issue, begging her not to ever divulge it to Anthony or anyone else.

Two weeks later, she got a new job as a clerk/cashier at a Shell gas station. It was a fifteen-minute drive, but she had saved up to buy a fairly used Nissan Maxima to get around town and go to doctor's appointments. Almost immediately, Nadia became a favorite of the customers. Her manager often commended her work ethic and attitude, but Nadia didn't let it all go to her head, especially the customers who always picked her out to issue their lottery tickets. Either by coincidence or whatever reason, they always won whenever they bought from her so much so that some customers would buy a two hundred and a fifty-dollar roll of tickets at a time. Nadia found it funny that they considered her a good luck charm, but she played along with them anyway.

Even at three months, she wasn't showing any bump, which she loved because she wouldn't have to start buying maternity clothes till later on. She sometimes got offers for dates but politely declined all, telling them sometimes that she was married. Until an unforgettable stranger walked into her life one evening.

It wasn't a particularly busy day. The manager was out, and the other cashier was stocking coolers in the back. As customary when it wasn't busy, Nadia was straightening displays on the shelf when he walked in. He was tall, about six foot two, in jeans and a white T-shirt, which did not take away from his magnificent physique at all. He carried a gym bag, and she suspected he probably just finished working out at the nearby popular Total Fit gym a few blocks from the gas station. A flutter welled in her stomach, but she attributed it to the baby, unwilling to admit to herself that she was attracted to another man so soon after Anthony.

He walked slowly to the back, picked a can of Arizona, and walked to the front. Nadia slowly walked behind him to the register. She had to crane up her neck to look up at him. He was not the most handsome man she had ever seen, but there was just something about him that ruffled her feathers in a nice way. His eyes were squint-like, almost piercing in their intensity as they gazed at her. His brows were bushy but only added to that raw look she liked.

"Will that be all?" she asked. "Any lottery tickets today?"

"No, just the tea." His deep, guttural voice sent shivers down her spine. "How are you today?" He smiled to reveal two perfect rows of white teeth with one gold incisor in the upper row. It should have marred an otherwise beautiful smile. Even though she detested gold teeth, she didn't care in this instance.

"Fine." She hoped her hands didn't shake as she rang up his purchase and gave him change. Their fingers connected briefly as she handed him the money, suffusing her body with warmth such as she had never felt. She wondered if he felt it, too.

"Thanks, Nadia." He read her name on the tag. "See you later."

"Bye," Nadia watched as he went out the door to a red Corvette, got in, and revved the engine. Just before he drove away, he turned his head toward the door, and they locked eyes. Then he was gone.

She couldn't get him off her mind as much as she tried to, and she longed for him to come into the store again, but he didn't. She couldn't fathom why she obsessed over a mere stranger, but her body betrayed her whenever he came to mind. His nice frame, his long legs, his gold-toothed smile, even the nice shape of his fingers were hard to forget, and she didn't deny herself her feelings at all. Life was meant to be lived, and what good was it if one couldn't revel in positive feelings, she surmised.

The pregnancy treated her well because she escaped the accompanying morning sickness, sleepiness, and fatigue. She took good care of herself just as her doctor suggested and was happy when the ultrasound showed the baby was a boy.

Around the fourth month, the pregnancy started showing, but she never missed any scheduled workdays, and even found it invigorating to be able to move around because of the nature of her job. The manager cautioned her to get help from her colleagues to lift heavy things, and even some of the customers started asking after her well-being. She was put on a rotating schedule which enabled her to work just two evenings a week, on Mondays and Tuesdays when the store was least likely to be busy, and not later than nine o clock in the night.

It was hard to predict customer flow, and so it was on this particular Tuesday night. It had been a slow night, but at eight thirty, it suddenly got busy in a flash. Nadia was manning the register for twenty minutes nonstop as customers went in and out of the store. She caught only a five-minute break and it suddenly became busy again. There were only two of them in the store, the manager was not around, and her relief had called in that he was running late. When she looked at her watch again, it was already half past nine, and he still hadn't shown up. He then called at ten that he couldn't make it because his car broke down on the way to work. The manager was away at a conference and the assistant manager said he wouldn't be able to come in because he was babysitting his children, but assured Nadia that a replacement would definitely be there at eleven. She had no choice but to stay. As her time to leave neared, she was glad when the string of customers finally trickled at quarter till. Her legs hurt, and she was tired as she rested her elbows on the counter, catching her breath, deep in thought.

"You all right?"

All her tiredness vanished at the deep voice. She straightened immediately. It was the stranger who had occupied her thoughts.

"I'm fine," she said.

His eyes squinted as they watched her. "You sure?"

"Yes."

He walked to the candy section, picked a pack of Doublemint and lay it on the counter. "Why are you working so late? I never see you here at this time."

"My relief didn't show," she said succinctly as she rang up his purchase. "Will that be all?"

"Yes," he said as he picked it up and left. "Thanks."

Nadia watched him leave with longing. She actually wished he could whisk her away at that moment. The pregnancy had been relatively easy, but lately she'd been feeling the extra weight, and the doctor had advised her not to stand for too long. It was with a sigh of relief that she picked up her bag and walked to her car after shift change, thanking God she was off on Wednesday. She walked slowly. She was so caught up in her thoughts that she didn't spot the Corvette or its owner as he left it and walked toward her. Just as she was about to get into her car, she heard her name.

"Nadia."

She turned around in astonishment, without an element of fear. Somehow, she just knew she felt safe in his presence. "Hey, hi!"

"Hi. Nick." He extended a hand. Their fingers touched, and deliciousness surged through her. He didn't let go soon enough as if he could feel it, too. "You're going home?"

"Yes." She retrieved her keys from her purse. "It's been a long day."

"I'll drive behind you."

"What?"

"I'll drive behind you. I'm not going to let you drive home by yourself at this time of night," he explained.

"You'll do no such thing!" she retorted. "I barely know you!"

"There's plenty of time," he said confidently, just as one of her colleagues walked toward them.

He cast an anxious look at Nadia. "Is everything OK?"

At that moment, Nadia knew she had two options. Say yes, and walk into her destiny, or say no, and probably never be bothered by Nick again. "I'm OK. Peter. He's a friend."

Peter looked at Nick suspiciously, then back at Nadia. "You sure?"

"Yes. Go on, Peter, you have customers waiting at the register." Nadia shooed. "I'm fine."

"All right. See you later then."

"They love you around here, huh?" Nick stated as Peter left. "You're very lucky."

Nadia shrugged. "You know they could have called the police?"

He shrugged, unshaken. "Why? For wanting to talk to a beautiful woman? Last time I heard it was still a free country. Now get in the car and I'll drive behind you, OK? Just to make sure you get home safe."

CHAPTER FOUR

It was almost midnight when they arrived at the apartment complex. Nick waited as she locked her car and followed her upstairs. All this was done in silence as if each knew what the other felt but was unwilling to voice it. His sure footsteps were reassuring as he walked behind her.

She stopped and turned to him when they got to the door. "Thank you—"

His head swooped down, and his lips locked with hers in a passionate kiss. He took his time, exploring her lips gently while he held her close to him. She caught a faint scent of musk and wood in his cologne. He would have continued if she hadn't broken the kiss.

"Nick—"

"Sorry, am I holding you too tight?" he released her slowly.

"No, God." Both of them were visibly dazed by the kiss. "Do you normally go round kissing pregnant women? I mean, a man could have come out that door and given you a good kick in the neck!" For all that she was feeling, Nadia tried to maintain control of the situation.

He leaned against the rail, breathing heavily. "Would you believe me if I told you I've never done that before in my life?" His back was to her. She saw his hands tighten. "I just had to kiss you, Nadia. God, what have you done to me?"

"That still does give you an excuse to kiss me like that, though. For all you know I could be married."

"Look, I'm really sorry," he said remorsefully. "I should have had more control. Really, I am sorry."

His look as he faced her was full of concern, such that Nadia decided to put him out of his misery. "I feel the same way, too," she said slowly.

He turned, and his eyes focused on her belly. "I usually don't go around kissing pregnant women, to answer your question. But where's the other person in this equation though? I don't think you're the kind of woman that would go around kissing other men while pregnant with another man's child, either."

"He's not in the picture."

"Why?"

"It's a long story." She shivered lightly, and he suggested they go in the apartment. She became hesitant. After all, she still barely knew him.

"I don't think that's a good idea."

"All right. I would have been alarmed if you did let me in. Come here." He kissed her lightly on the lips. "You're working tomorrow?"

"No."

"Good. I'll pick you up at six pm."

"Nick—"

"Now, go on. Make sure you lock the door. I'll stand here," he said firmly, dismissing any protest from her. His eyes were tender as he looked at her.

Nadia nodded, smiled, and locked the door behind her. She stayed on the other side of the door, exhilarated yet confused by what just happened, and only moved when she heard his footsteps descend the stairs five minutes later.

He picked her up promptly at six the next day, clad in jeans and a blue plaid shirt with rolled sleeves. He looked so good she couldn't help but gasp in surprise.

"I don't want to go anywhere too fancy," she said in the car.

"Where would you like? By the way, you look really nice." He swept her appearance appreciatively as she sat next to him in the

Corvette. Her gown was a simple burgundy A-line, paired with espadrilles, and garnet stud earrings.

"Thank you. I don't know…my appetite fluctuates these days. Sometimes I eat a lot, sometimes less, but I've developed a thing for the Taco Cabana fajita bowl. It's just weird. I never really used to eat it, and my roommate brought me one day, and it's all I want to eat all the time."

He laughed. "Chicken or beef?"

"What do you think?" she replied feistily. "I'm a beef kind of gal."

"I believe that," he concurred. "So, you have a roommate?"

He drove the car with such ease Nadia couldn't help but flush as she remembered their kiss from the night before. He had kissed her with the same ease, too.

"Yes, Liz, kind of my best friend, too. She has been my rock through this pregnancy."

And there was silence after that. Nadia knew she was embarking on another journey by agreeing to this date with Nick, but in a way, she was tired of being the "good girl" all the time. She was tired of playing it safe and denying herself the good times she deserved, be it in relationships or life. She decided to stay in the United States so she could enjoy some freedom, the restriction on her life in Nigeria ever in her subconscious, and opportunities would be missed if she said no to every blessing that came her way.

They soon found a restaurant. She ordered a beef fajita bowl while Nick settled for two chicken tacos and iced tea. But they didn't eat at the restaurant. Instead, he took her to a park near the restaurant.

"I like the quietness of this park. I come here whenever I can to unwind when I'm not at the gym."

"Do you work out a lot?"

"At least three to five times a week. I like to keep in shape. I sit behind a desk most of the time so any opportunity I get to work out is heaven."

"What do you do?" she asked as they ate their meals. "You don't look like somebody who sits behind a desk."

"Really? Trust me, appearances can be deceiving. I, myself, never thought I'd ever adapt to the desk until the little software company I developed in college exploded and turned into a million-dollar corporation, thanks to the demand for cybersecurity."

"Really?"

"Yes. Wow. That was what I said when the contracts first came pouring in. You may have heard of us: KNG Corporation. We were featured in the most influential companies in Houston list last month in *EQ* magazine. I declined to have my picture on the cover for obvious reasons. I value my privacy a lot."

Nadia listened, enraptured as he told her about himself, his family, his business, and his passion for mentoring others to succeed. All with such humility that she fell more in love with him as the night wore on. The park's visitors had turned from raucous families to lovers and older couples as they strolled beneath the serene trees, surrounded by warm evening lights. So much so that she was flustered when he suddenly stopped and looked deep into her eyes.

"Now tell me about yourself."

"What do you want to know?"

"Everything, including this," he placed a hand on her stomach, flustering her. "Where is this foolish man who would leave a beautiful woman like you by yourself when you are carrying his child?"

It was more a statement than a question, and she could feel the controlled anger in his voice. It was only their first date, but she felt so comfortable with Nick already. So, she told him about her life in Nigeria, her travel to the United States, about Ben and Florence, about her previous job at the restaurant, about her roommates, and about Anthony.

"So, he invited you down to Houston only allowed you stay a day with him, handed you over to some roommates, decided to take advantage of you on a booty call, and then became incommunicado? That's very strange," Nick observed. "Maybe there's more to the story."

"I don't know, Nick. He never picked up my calls or called me back. But I don't harbor any ill feelings toward him, though. I don't think it's fair to say that he took advantage of me. I was a willing participant, and I don't think anything happened that I didn't want.

This baby, though, is mine, and I will take care of him and nurture him and make him into a real gentleman." She rubbed her stomach with tenderness. "I love him so much already."

There was a strange look on Nick's face as he watched her. "And you're going to do it alone, all by yourself?"

"Of course! I can take care of myself."

"I could help out, you know."

"How?"

He shrugged, placing his hands on hers. The baby fluttered at that moment, shocking both of them. "Oh my God! Did the baby just move?"

"Yes!" Nadia couldn't contain her excitement. "That's the first time I ever felt him move. Oh my God!"

She couldn't help herself as she hugged Nick, then burst into tears as she became overwhelmed by the moment. He held her tenderly as she let her emotions reign. Soon, after, they left the park and he dropped her off at home.

They went on several dates after that, and the more they saw of each other, the more Nadia became attached to him. He was always at her beck and call despite his busy schedule. With him by her side, and Liz, Nadia soon started slowly pushing Anthony out her of mind. She was very happy, although she was reluctant to tell her parents about the baby. She didn't think they would understand how she got herself in that situation, and she also didn't want to cause problems between her family and the Okafors.

That park, however, became their favorite place to go, and they spent many hours there just enjoying each other's company. So, when Nick called out of the blue one evening to ask if she would like to go out to the park, she didn't refuse though she was tired from work. She needed a breath of fresh air anyway.

It was a nice Sunday evening, and the park was less crowded than usual. As usual, she didn't hesitate when Nick pulled her into his arms. She lay her had on his chest, listening to the reassuring rhythm of his heart.

"Nadia, marry me."

Her head shot up in astonishment. "What did you say?"

He held her away from him, looking deep into her eyes. "Marry me. Look, I know we come from totally different backgrounds, but I know I can't let you out of my life with the way I feel about you. Since that first day, I just couldn't get you out of my mind. I thought it was temporary, but the more I thought about you, the more I wanted to see you. I avoided coming to the gas station when you were there, but I just couldn't hold back anymore. I love you, Nadia. Let me take care of you and the baby."

"But this is another man's child," she reiterated. "What would your family think?"

"They are reasonable people, and they want me to be happy, which is the most important thing. I even told my mom about you two days ago. She can't wait to meet you."

"Oh my God." Nadia couldn't take it in. It was too soon, too much, and too lifechanging. What would her family think? How could she jump from being pregnant and being abandoned by Anthony to meeting Nick and getting married all within the space of six months? They certainly wouldn't be happy about her being pregnant for Anthony, but this? Getting married to Nick? the thought was crazy as it was. "You don't have to marry me, Nick. We can go out if you want, but not marriage."

"Think. Look at it as killing two birds with one stone. I love you, you love me, and I'll even help you get your residency."

"You don't have to marry me for that, Nick. What will you be getting out of this? A pregnant bride and the child's not yours?"

"Stop it, Nadia. I know I'll be getting the most caring, compassionate, considerate, beautiful woman on Earth, whom I also love very much. Come here." He kissed her long and hard. "I love you so much. Say yes?"

"Give me a couple of days to think about it."

"Two days."

"One week."

"Three days."

"Deal."

He gathered their leftovers and threw them in a nearby trash can. "Let me get you back home."

Nadia swore Lizzy always surprised her with her logic. The first thing she did on hearing about Nick's proposal was to dance around the tiny apartment, then give Nadia a tight hug, before telling her to go for it.

"What? I'd have thought you'd be telling me to run the other way!"

"Do I look like I'm stupid? The guy loves you, and he wants to marry you despite the pregnancy, and you'll be getting your green card. What better thing could happen than this? Please be smart, Nadia. And he's very rich, too. God has buttered your bread."

"You're crazy, Liz."

"You'll be the one who's crazy not to marry this guy. I want to meet him, though. He sounds too good to be true. Heck, I am surprised I haven't met him!"

"We're meeting on Saturday. He's taking me to meet his parents, depending on my answer. You won't be here in the evening since you're working."

"Trust me, this is too good to pass up. I will definitely wait to meet him before I go to work. This is crucial," Lizzy said. "But if it's true, I'm so happy for you, girl." She gave Nadia a big hug. "See how God works?"

"I'm still in shock."

"Don't be, girl. Just when you least expect it, the Lord shows up and fixes our pain. He never forgets His own."

True to her word, Lizzy did wait to meet Nick on Saturday, and Nadia could see she was indeed impressed. She watched in silence as Lizzy lectured him on how precious Nadia was and what was going to happen if he as much as let a follicle be blocked on her head. They all laughed and bid her goodbye as they left for his parents' house.

"Feisty, ain't she?' he quipped in the car. "I like her."

"Nobody has a choice in liking Liz. You either take it or leave it. She comes across as hard but with the most beautiful heart. I don't know what I would have done without her."

"That's because you yourself are good too, Nadia. You make it easy to be liked, and helped, and to be loved."

"So, you love me?"

"With all my heart," he said seriously, taking her hand briefly. "And the baby, too."

Nick's parents lived in the posh Houston neighborhood of River Oaks in Harris County. It wasn't only them at home, though, when they got there. Nick's younger sister Keira was there, as well as the youngest son Kenneth, and their aunt Lorraine. Humbleness did run in the family, Nadia discovered as the night wore on. A lot of questions were asked especially about her background, and they didn't seem to mind that she was from Nigeria.

"You are as cute as any American girl I've seen," Lorraine commented. "Wow, and you carry pregnancy well. Is it a boy? Come here." She walked around Nadia, examining her critically. "I can tell it's a boy. Look how it's sitting."

"How it's sitting?" Nick's mom couldn't contain her laughter. "Lorraine, leave the girl alone. How do you know it's a boy or a girl?"

"I tell you, it's a boy. It's a boy, isn't it?" Lorraine persisted.

"Leave my girl alone, Aunt Lorraine." Nick saved the day by putting his arm on her shoulder. "It's a boy, satisfied?"

"I say!" Lorraine shouted. "I'm never wrong about these things. That's how we do it in those days. Don't need no doctor to tell me I'm having a boy or a girl. Seven children in total."

They all laughed as they went into the dining room, where a feast of roast chicken, braised lamb, endless vegetables, fruits, desserts, and three kinds of wines was waiting. Nadia was comfortable as they joked and made fun of Nick and his childhood antics amidst all his protests. Nadia fell in love with the family just as she had fallen in love with him. She couldn't be happier, and it was almost reluctantly that she got up later when Nick said it was time to go.

"Both of you can stay," Nick's mother prompted. "We have enough rooms."

"It's OK, Mom. We'll come by and see you soon," he promised.

"Don't let it be too long."

"I promise. Thanks for the food, Mom." He kissed his mom. "Dad." He gave his dad a hug. "Thanks for everything."

"Proud of you, son. Take good care of her, all right?"

"Yes, Dad," he said as they said goodbyes to the others and left. "Did you enjoy yourself?" he asked as soon as they entered the car. "You must be tired."

"I am, but your family is so down to earth, Nick. I am really glad I said yes."

"We don't need to have an elaborate ceremony. I already told my parents we can get a marriage certificate and be married in three days. And you have to quit your job."

"Noooo, that's one thing I can't do, Nick. I love my job, if I quit, then I must get something else."

"You can come work with me."

Nadia noted that he used "with" instead of "for." At that moment, she realized how lucky she was to have Nick in her life. "I love you, Nick."

"And I love you. I'll take you to the office on Monday. I think we have a current opening for an administrative assistant position in the personnel department. If you want that. If not, I can arrange something else."

"No, that's fine, and I also want to enroll in college."

"Soon as the baby is born, we'll take care of that. One step at a time. I can't wait to make you Mrs. Nick Gardner."

"And I can't wait to make an honest man of you, Mr. Gardner," she replied. They both laughed, reveling in the love and warmth between them.

They were married a week later at the courthouse in Downtown Houston. Lizzy and one of Nick's friends were present as witnesses. They all went to Mark's American Cuisine on Westheimer for lunch. It was a very expensive restaurant, but Nadia liked it and she was slowly getting used to being spoiled by Nick anyway.

They finally were able to be by themselves at two in the afternoon. Lizzy had to go to work, and Nick's friend had a plane to catch. On the way home, Nadia got the craving for beef fajita bowl, and they made a stop at Taco Cabana.

"Let's go to the park," she suggested.

"Now? I want to spend some time with my wife," Nick said.

"You have all night, love. Come on." She persuaded him that she needed the fresh air, and they found themselves in the same park he had proposed, sitting on the same bench. "I love this place."

"You do?" Nick watched affectionately as she munched on taco shells. "I can't believe you're eating again, after all, that food at Mark's."

Nadia patted her stomach. "Remember, I'm eating for two. Mark's was the baby's food, now its's my turn to eat. Hmm." She licked her finger seductively. "You want some?"

"Keep doing that, and I hope we don't spend the night in jail for public indecency. You're just so genuine, Nadia. Please don't ever change." He kissed her on the lips, not minding the taco sauce. "I love you, Mrs. Gardner."

"Thanks for everything," she said, playing with the diamond ring on her finger. She had protested when she saw the price, but he wouldn't have it any other way. The cost alone could have paid her waitress salary for three whole years.

"What for? Any man who would leave you for whatever reason must be crazy. Besides," his voice dropped suggestively. "I can't wait to get you in my bed."

"Nick!"

"Yes, love. Haven't I tried, keeping my hands off you all this while? There's only so much a man can take."

"So, you married me just to have your way with me?"

"God forbid, that alone is not enough to hold my attention. Nadia, you're everything I've ever wanted in a woman with a nice behind to boot."

"Geez, you're spoiled rotten, Mr. Gardner, talking to your wife like that."

"Case in point, wife, underlined. You're so beautiful. Aunt Lorraine was right. Pregnancy does become you. You're glowing so positively." He drew her to him in a long kiss, eliciting cheers and claps from some passersby. "I think we need to get a room."

"Yes," Nadia was dazed by the kiss. She couldn't wait to be one with him. "Let's go, love," they hastily packed up their leftovers and they went home.

The next two months was a whirlwind as Nadia settled into married life, in addition to securing a job at KNG Corporation,

Nick's company. She was only one of four employees in the personnel department. The human resources manager was a big woman in her early sixties called Bettie, who spoke gruffly like a man and would not be caught dead in a dress.

"Dresses," she said, "Were invented just to slow us women down, and there ain't no slowing Bettie down." Just dresses, though, because she loved her pencil skirts, slimming with blouses and shirts neatly tucked. She was a stickler for time and hated to be kept waiting. She was very nice and jovial, though, and her husband Shannon frequented the office to pick her up for lunch almost every day.

Melinda, a pretty Hispanic in her mid-twenties, had been with the company for five years and acted as manager whenever Bettie was not around. She and Nadia hit it off immediately, especially as they were in the same age group. Melinda was in a volatile marriage to a man called Benito, who Nadia suspected was abusive because Melinda sometimes came to work with red puffy eyes, though she would never admit to what was going on. Nadia minded her own business, but she vowed to herself that the day Melinda came to the office with a blue or black eye, she was telling Nick about it, especially as the couple had two little children.

Debbie was strictly in charge of recruitment. She was the most blackish white girl Nadia had ever seen. She actually thought Debbie was black when she spoke with her on the phone, only to be perplexed when she saw her in person. Debbie loved corn-rowing her hair, listening to rap music, and was the nicest person Nadia had ever come across. Debbie had the knack for making difficult things seemed nonexistent. Nadia could go to her with any problem, and it would be solved or, at least, half-solved by the time she was done with it. It was no wonder. She was actually a math whiz and had graduated with top honors in accounting from the University of Houston,-Clear Lake, with an MBA from Rice University to top it off. Bettie might be the manager, but Debbie was the glue that held the personnel office together. Nadia had no doubt that Debbie would get the job human resources manager job once Bettie retired in five years' time, if another company did not snatch her before then. But then, Nick paid his employees very well.

Debbie was also a foodie and had introduced Nadia to some really nice quirky restaurants in Houston, as she didn't mind driving an hour to go for lunch. The personnel office's hours were very flexible as long as an employee put in the minimum of eight hours for each shift each day.

Nadia was basically a clerk, handling correspondence, filing, and mailing distribution, in addition to helping out the others when they needed extra hands. She loved the job, though, and it was way better than her jobs at the gas station and Mimi's Restaurant. Her salary was twice the going rate for the position. She was even happier to discover that her predecessor had earned the same salary, dispelling her belief that she was paid so much because she was Nick's wife.

Nadia usually came to work at eight and worked until five, taking only a half hour break anytime between twelve and one. She liked bringing her lunch and mingling with other staff in the cafeteria also though some of them had no idea she was married to the owner of the company, which suited her just fine. She also cautioned Nick about coming to get her for lunch. They would meet at a designated place and drive in their separate cars, which Debbie found odd but quaint.

She couldn't have asked for a more perfect man. He was always attentive to her needs, followed her to doctor's appointments whenever he was not too busy at the office, and surprised her with roses and gifts ever so often. Before she met him, she never thought that a woman could have so much in life and not in terms of material things at all.

They decorated the nursery together, shopped for the baby together, and he even commissioned an artist to render a portrait of her, which turned out so good he had a second one made to hang in a private room in his office.

He catered to her every want and need, including helping her family back home in Nigeria. Her father certainly didn't mind that Nick was a Christian when a brand-new Toyota Sienna was shipped to him, nor when he received money to build a shelter and gate in the front yard of the bungalow to update the space that was now being used as a neighborhood mosque on Seventh Street.

It had not been easy to tell her parents about her marriage to Nick, but they had done it together, over the phone, and her parents' fears had been put to rest after hearing Nick and his assurances that she was well taken care of. If possible, they might have even known how much he loved her from the way he talked about her.

Nadia considered herself very lucky to have Nick in her life, and she never once doubted his love for her. Initially it had been rough; Nick, being the man that he was, of course had previous relationships, and his immediate ex before he met her didn't really believe that relationship had ended. The landline in the house had to be changed because she kept calling insulting Nadia and telling her to go back to Africa. All the locks had to be changed too, but eventually she got the message and left them alone. As for her parents, they became so fond of Nick that they just called him direct whenever they needed anything. And her father, who was not too thrilled that Nick was not a Muslim initially, was already picking out Muslim names for the boy.

The office had been busy earlier but had quieted down as lunch hour approached. Nadia was already in her thirty-third week and she couldn't wait to have the baby already. She had gained almost twenty-five pounds on her slender frame, which delighted Nick to no end especially in bed. She practically blushed when she remembered the night before.

"Whatever you're thinking, it must be good." This from Bettie as she walked into the office with two bags of Burger King and tossed her one. "I got your favorite, a Whopper and a Sprite." She placed the drink on Nadia's desk. "So, what were you thinking? Might I be wrong to think it has to do with Mr. Gardner himself?" she teased.

Nadia tossed a fry in her mouth. "Uh-huh, private business."

"All right. All right," she said gruffly and went to her desk, going into boss mode immediately. "Did you send out those letters to the shortlisted candidates for the IT coder job?"

"Yes, they went out with the afternoon mail. And I copied all the applications to the IT manager, too."

"Thanks, Nadia. Also, send an email to Nick as he will be sitting in the interview, too. He already knows the date and times."

"OK," Nadia said. "Your husband called. He'll be home late today. Too many requests coming in because of the summer heat."

Shannon was the manager at a popular HVAC company, and they had been inundated with work since the beginning of summer. Houston's heat could be dangerous when caught unawares, and it was not fun at all to have the air conditioner stop work in the middle of ninety-degree heat.

"Tell me about it, every summer we go through this, I've told him to quit that job and go easy, but nooo, he wants to work till he's eighty!"

Nadia laughed. "He does love his job, Bettie, and it keeps him going and young for you, yes?"

Bettie harrumphed loudly. "He certainly doesn't need the money."

Melinda walked in with Debbie at that moment with a box of Shipley Donuts.

"Don't ask me," Debbie said. "It's Melinda here who had a craving for sugar. Methinks she's pregnant."

"Really?" both Nadia and Bettie exclaimed. Bettie in surprise, Nadia more in shock. Just two days ago the poor girl had come in with bruises on her arm, which she attributed to a fall. Nadia knew better, though, and she didn't understand why she would go and have another baby for Benito.

"Congratulations!" she said, giving Melinda a long look. It might be time to tell Nick what was going on, at least for the baby's sake.

After work, Nadia stopped by the post office to pick up a box of Nigerian goodies that had been sent by her family. The local African store kept a good stock of native food, but some of them just didn't taste like back home. Among other things, she had gotten a big jar of pepper soup spice, which she couldn't wait to make for Nick. She had gradually introduced him to spicy food. He wasn't there yet, but he was relatively better than when they first met when the slightest bit of spice made him run for the river. One day, she had watched in obvious sympathy as he ran to the fridge after eating spicy bean cake she bought at the African store. She just couldn't help laughing as he danced around, holding his mouth and cussing like a sailor, vowing never to eat anything spicy again.

"A little bit of spice won't kill you, Nick. In fact, it boosts your immune system," she advised.

"Really." He looked at her doubtfully. "I hope that baby won't come out craving packs of ice with all that spicy stuff you're eating."

"I'm perfectly fine." The banter between them was healthy and open. He was certainly her best friend, and she could tell him anything.

She got into the shower as soon as she got home, hot and sticky from the heat even with her light gown. The cold water was revitalizing, so much so that time passed without her knowing. By the time she got out, it was almost sixty thirty, and there was no sign of Nick. She thought about calling him but shrugged off his lateness to something at the office and went downstairs to prepare dinner.

The house was a modest three-bedroom townhouse in the Galleria area, close to work and not far from downtown. Nick bought it right after he finished college, and it was full of bachelor furniture when she first came. She had since redecorated it to feature contemporary rustic furniture in the living room, updated draperies, and remodeled the kitchen more to her taste. Nick had given her a carte blanche to do as she pleased, but she surprised even herself by finishing below budget.

She was in one of his shirts as she rummaged around the kitchen looking for ingredients to make Scotch eggs to go with the left over fried rice from the previous night.

The baby had been kicking more than usual lately, and she had to stop sometimes to catch her breath. It was times like this that she liked Nick being around because he loved to help her cook, which usually led to other things afterward.

She glanced at the microwave clock, alarmed that it was eight and he wasn't still home. This was very unusual, as he would have called to let her know. Slowly, she made her way upstairs to the bedroom to retrieve her cell phone from her bag. There was a total of twenty missed calls, none from Nick's number. She scrolled the call log frantically. Several calls from his parents, some from Keira and Kenneth, and even some from Lorraine. Panic set in as she quickly dialed his mother's number.

Somehow, she knew he wouldn't answer if she called his phone. Tears were already streaming down her face as she heard his mother's broken voice at the other end. The phone slipped slowly from her as she tried to decipher what was being said. Her heart raced, her world started turning dark, and the last thing she remembered was falling slowly to the floor and not even feeling the impact.

When Nadia finally came to, she noticed that she was in a hospital room. Everybody was at her side except Nick, and she had given birth to little a baby boy she later named Emmett Nick Gardner.

Nick's family and Lizzy tried as much as they could to keep Nadia emotionally grounded so she could take care of the baby, but it was a rough first three months for Emmett. Even though Nadia vowed to only breastfeed the first six months, she had to resort to pumping breast milk for him because she just couldn't handle the sadness. However, with time, she regained herself, though Nick was always on her mind. He had been her knight in shining armor, and his loss would forever leave a hole in her heart. She didn't even know if she could possibly love another man after Nick. Only Emmett occupied her heart, and to her he was Nick's son and would forever be. Anthony had receded to nothing in her heart long time ago. To her, he simply didn't exist.

CHAPTER FIVE

It was late when Nadia left the office. KNG Corporation was in the process of acquiring a small-scale software company with very good prospects, and the acquisition was proving more than difficult. The CEO wanted to be part of the board at KNG Corporation and still retain his current position. Nadia, on the other hand, wanted him to head the new sales department just established in order to push sales, especially for the innovative software. Kenneth, Nick's brother, felt they should give in to his demands before he sold out to another larger corporation, and there had been endless meetings with no recourse on a mutual agreement. It was taxing, to say the least, but she was used to it, having spent the past fifteen years learning the ropes from veteran employees at the company Nick left her upon his death.

The first few years hadn't been easy. When she woke up at the hospital that fateful night and Nick was not there, she knew her worst nightmare had come to pass. She was told later that she had been in so much pain that doctors had to do a C-section to make sure the baby did not come to harm amidst her grief.

Nick had left the office just like any other evening and was just ten minutes from home when his car was hit head-on by a wayward minivan with failed brakes. The young mother and her two children survived, although she would never be able to walk again.

Nadia would have given anything to have Nick back, not minding a wheelchair or walking stick or any loss of limbs. Anything, but the vast emptiness she felt at losing him at the moment that life was as its best for both of them. His lovemaking had been so tender the previous night, and he had held her close until morning, waking her up at dawn not to make love but just to talk to her. He had told her how grateful and thankful he was to have her in his life, his hopes for the future, and how excited he was at the impending arrival of the baby in a couple of weeks.

He left work before her after a perfunctory kiss on the check and a playful slap on her derriere with a promise from her to call him if she needed anything. Little did they know that would be the last time they would see each other.

The other driver did not have insurance, and Nadia ended up paying medical bills for her and the children because she was a single mom, and then hired her to work in personnel after she left to head KNG Corporation. Everybody thought she was crazy, but she knew that was what Nick would have wanted. The accident was a mechanical failure and why cause more grief when a life had already been lost? Tammy proved to be a very good employee and was now the second-in-command in personnel next to Melinda, who got the manager position after Bettie retired. Debbie was promoted to Chief Financial Officer, and together with Kenneth who was the Vice President, there couldn't have been a better team to move the company forward.

Nick's family had been Nadia's rock through those turbulent years. His parents moved in with her for a while to help with the baby and also helped her bring Rakhya to the United States. Rakhya was thirty-five now, married with three children, and a nurse at MD Anderson Cancer Center in Houston, one of the largest cancer centers in the United States.

Nadia missed Nick every day though the pain had lessened a little bit. He came into her thoughts mostly at night, when the night was cold and the warmth of the blankets was not enough to comfort her tears, tears she shed only when alone and which turned to tears of joy when her thoughts shifted to Emmett, who was now fifteen and her source of solace. She could never hide anything from him.

As soon as he was old enough, she had explained the circumstances surrounding his birth to him, telling him about both Nick and Anthony. She made sure he spent a lot of time with Nick's family so he could be well-grounded like the men, and it paid off. Emmett was well-behaved, an honors student at school, and a super athlete on the football field. Even at fifteen, he was making a name for himself in high school football, and his coaches had hinted that colleges might come calling earlier for him than usual. His last name was Gardner. Nadia wouldn't have it any other way. Nick had loved him even before he was born, and keeping the last name forged a closer tie with the family. They treated Emmett just as they would their own grandchild without any hesitation.

As Nadia drove home, on a whim, she stopped by at the gas station where she used to work, and she had met Nick to buy gas. The store had changed a lot. It was bigger, and Peter was now the manager. Nostalgia hit her as she waited by the cash register, and she shrugged it off and left. Rakhya called just as Nadia was parking in front of the house. She had purchased a nice four-bedroom house at Sienna Plantation in Missouri City after she couldn't stand being in the house she had shared with Nick by herself. "Hi, Rakhya."

"Hi, sis," Rakhya said. "Just calling to check on you. How is Emmett? Are you at home?"

"Just getting home. I'm still in the car. Emmett is fine. How are your hubby and kids?"

"Good, I was wondering if we could stop by on Sunday after church." Rakhya had converted to Christianity after meeting her husband, a staunch Baptist, during her master's program at the Houston Baptist University.

Nadia knew she needed the company. Emmett doted on his three cousins though they drove him crazy half of the time. "Why not? That would be nice. Is it only you and the kids, or all of you, so I can know what to make for dinner?"

"You don't need to make a feast, Nadia. Yes, all of us. We should be there around two thirty."

"All right then. Kiss the children for me," Nadia said.

"Sure, sis. See ya." Rakhya hung up.

Nadia spent a couple of minutes in the car, deep in thought, and didn't notice Emmett until he knocked on the window.

"You OK, Mom?"

"Yes, how have you been?"

"Good," Emmett shrugged. "Practice was canceled today because the weather was too hot. We might have to make up on Saturday, though. Aunt Lorraine is here."

"Really?" Nadia smiled. "Hope my fridge is still intact."

Emmett shook his head. "She made dinner. Greens, cornbread, fried chicken, and mashed potatoes. You know how she is."

"Indeed." But Nadia was glad Lorraine was around. She loved Emmett to death and didn't mind staying at the house when Nadia traveled, which became more frequent as she took on more responsibilities at KNG Corporation. They practically raised Emmett together. What's more, she was funny and there was never a dull moment in her presence.

Nadia considered herself blessed, but lately, something else had been gnawing at her. The need for human contact, for a tender touch, and the need to look into another's eyes and see unconditional love reflected back.

Anthony still came to mind now and then, but memories of him were fleeting. She got news about him from Lizzy from time to time and how well he was doing at his law firm. He had gone back to school to study law and was doing quite well, too. Last Nadia heard, he and the family traveled to Nigeria for Nkechi's wedding. Kate, the sister who never liked her, had been in the United States for a while now with her family also, and though they lived in the same subdivision, she and Nadia had never crossed paths. She really didn't want to see any of them, though, if she had a choice. She wondered how odd it was that in fifteen years she never as much as bumped into Anthony anywhere, though she sometimes saw him and his wife photographed at parties in some Nigerian magazines.

Her thoughts were cut short by Lorraine who was still in an apron with a ladle in her hand, coming from the kitchen.

"Nadia!" She enclosed her in a bear hug as the server nearly missed her cheek. "How are you? I've made dinner, girl. So, you just go upstairs and change and come down to eat."

"Lorraine, nice to see you." Nadia laughed, "I can see you've helped yourself to my kitchen again."

"You know me, girl," Lorraine laughed. "I just couldn't wait to see my Munchkin." That was her nickname for Emmett. "Also, it's been too long."

Nadia could feel Lorraine's eyes on her as they relaxed, watching TV after dinner. Emmett had gone to bed as he had early practice in the morning.

"You can just come out and say it, Lorraine. I know something's on your mind."

"Yes, Nadia, I do have something on my mind. Isn't it time you moved on and found somebody to share life with?"

"Lorraine!"

Morayode

"Yes, Nadia, look, it's been fifteen years. You have done well with the company and raised a good son, but you can't go on like this, living in this big house all by yourself," Lorraine pointed out.

"I live with Emmett," Nadia reminded her.

"Who will soon graduate from high school and go to college, then what will you do? The family's worried about you. We know you loved Nick very much, but it's time you moved on. He would have wanted you to be happy."

It was true. After Nick's death, she devoted all her time to KNG Corporation and raising Emmett, but she had been thinking how lonely she felt lately. She hadn't gone on a date in fifteen years, and she would definitely like to have at least one more child before she was forty.

"Thanks, Lorraine, I know you guys have my well-being at heart, but I haven't met the right person to take Nick's place."

"Nadia!" Lorraine turned to her. "Look at me, girl. Nobody, and I say, nobody would ever take Nick's place in your heart. You need to find a man that will occupy the void in your heart, not necessarily take his place because love will always be love. You just need to make an extra space."

"OK, Lorraine, I'll try," Nadia said. "I really appreciate your concern."

She dropped Lorraine off on her way to work the next day after a promise to see her in two weeks' time. She was almost running late for another meeting with the representatives of the software company, and the headstrong CEO was there too, ready to battle.

100 | Page

By the time they emerged from the conference room at eleven, however, the deal had been sealed to both parties' satisfaction.

Nadia couldn't wait to go celebrate with an early lunch at Pappadeaux seafood restaurant and was on her way out the door when her office phone rang. It was Lizzy.

"Hey Nadia," she said in her characteristic jovial voice. "How's it going?"

"Liz, good to hear from you girl. How's the family?"

"Good. How's Emmett doing? He was mentioned on the news the other day. You must be very proud of him."

"I am, Liz. He is the light of my life," Nadia stated. "Are you at work?" Lizzy worked as a probation officer for Harris County.

"I'm off today. Have you heard the news?"

"What news?"

"Anthony got divorced again."."

"What?" Nadia couldn't believe her ears. "You're kidding me."

"No, Angela told me herself."

"Wow!" Nadia was at a loss for words. "Anyway, I was on my way to lunch. I'll call you later, OK?"

"You don't have anything to say?"

"Liz, what could I possibly say? I wish him well."

"She gave him custody of the girls, too."

"What kind of woman would do that?" Nadia couldn't imagine being without Emmett for a day. "Why?"

"That woman is something else, Nadia. Apparently, she met another guy who doesn't have kids yet and feels the kids would hinder her new relationship. Oh God, some women. How does she know that it will last? Anthony was so good to her, too."

"Remember there are two sides to a story. After what Anthony did to me, I beg to differ, though I'm not bitter. I've got to go now. I'll call you later, Liz."

First Colony mall was packed, but Nadia didn't mind. Once in a while, she loved to unwind by shopping and splurging on herself, and this Saturday she woke up feeling really good especially with the acquisition deal finalized. Even the news that Anthony was divorced had no bearing on her mood.

After a light breakfast of a bagel and a cup of international coffee mocha, she got dressed and brought the Corvette out of the garage. The car was chock full of memories she would forever cherish, and she refused to sell it despite several offers from strangers whenever she drove it. Besides, it was well maintained, and she hoped to pass it on to Emmett for his sixteenth birthday, though he didn't know it yet.

Her first stop was H & M, then a little browsing inside Ross clothing store before she entered the Apple Store to see if she could get the latest iPhone. She was a Samsung girl, but she'd heard so many raves from her colleagues about the wonderful features on the phone and it would also be an opportunity to get Emmett an Apple watch. He'd hinted several times about it, and she pretended not to hear, so it would be a nice surprise for him. She was waylaid by a salesgirl as soon as she entered the store, and if nothing else the excellent customer service delighted her to no end.

She ended up buying both products and was walking out the door when two girls came in, laughing excitedly as they passed her. There was something familiar about one of the girls' laugh, and she stopped for a moment to look back at them, trying to recollect, when she accidently bumped into a solid body.

"Oh, sorry!" she exclaimed as strong hands came out to steady her. "Oh my God!" she gasped as she saw his face. "Anthony!"

"Hi, Nadia," he said as if also shocked to see her. "Nadia!" For several minutes, they were oblivious to everything around them as their eyes locked in brief eternity.

"Daddy!" one of the teenagers, the one with the familiar laugh, was at Anthony's side, "You coming?" She watched both adults in askance. "Daddy!"

"Hold on, Erin. I'll be right with you. Where's your sister?"

"Checking out iPhones."

"OK. I'll be with you in a moment, OK?"

Erin cast a suspicious glance at Nadia as she walked away. Nadia wasn't surprised. She almost smiled at the girl's antics. She probably was still nursing the idea of her parents getting back together, and if only she knew the little to no interest Nadia had in her daddy.

Anthony attempted a smile. "Kids. Nadia—"

"Nice seeing you, Anthony. Bye." She quickly sidestepped him and walked away.

"Nadia!"

She didn't look back and was determined for the incident not to ruin her shopping mood. She made two more purchases before leaving the mall and didn't allow her thoughts to wander until she made a stop at HEB to pick up groceries in preparation for Rakhya's visit on Sunday. She was surprised that she hadn't felt the tiny electric shocks she usually felt at his touch. Certainly, there was something during that moment when they gazed at each other, but it was more relaxed and warmer like old wine. She was surprised by the amount of gray in his hair, though it didn't take away from his good looks.

Sunday's visit went very well, and it was six when the visitors finally left. Emmett helped load the dishes in the dishwasher and then left to see a movie with a few friends. The house suddenly felt empty as Nadia sat alone in the living room. She understood now what Lorraine meant about how she would cope when Emmett went away to college. Anthony drifted in and out of her mind, as much as she tried to squelch the feeling he evoked in her. It wasn't hate, but she didn't like that there was not even an ounce of anger in her where he was concerned. It was more like he was just there, occupying a space devoid of feeling but refusing to go away.

She waited till Emmett came back at ten before going to bed. Sleep was sporadic, and she managed to catch a straight three hours before the alarm went off at six. After a fifteen-minute devotion praying and reading her Bible, she had a workout on the elliptical bike, a habit she picked up from Nick which had paid off well. She wasn't able to go to the gym, but the little she did every morning made a difference and prayer kept her grounded.

Her strict religious upbringing had caused her to rebel in such a way that she hadn't identified with any religion during her early years in the United States. However, after several personal experiences with God, she had converted to Christianity in the church she and Nick attended when she was pregnant. Nadia believed she was a good Christian but scoffed at making a big deal out of church attendance. She took Emmett to services a lot when he was younger but allowed him to find his own level as he got older. He had begun attending Sunday services at his best friend's church, and she didn't mind dropping him off when he couldn't find a ride.

There were several messages waiting for her at the office. Mondays were hectic so she usually designated Debbie to take care of issues that could be solved without her input. Two of the messages were from a so-called "David" who insisted that he wanted to speak with nobody else but her.

"I don't know, Nadia. He was pretty insistent. Wouldn't even tell me the nature of his call," Debbie said apologetically. "I tried."

"It's OK, Debbie. Thanks."

"Anytime," Debbie smiled, winking. "If he gives you a hard time, send him back to me."

Nadia laughed. "I'm sure it won't come to that, anyway. Thanks."

"You're welcome." Debbie left, shutting the door behind her.

Nadia looked at the messages again. Two from "David" and one from Bettie, who still called to check on her from time to time. Deciding to call Bettie later, she picked up the phone and called "David."

He picked up on the first ring, and after pleasantries explained that he operated an IT firm that contracted services out to various organizations in the Houston area. Two of the companies he serviced recently merged and needed tighter security for their client data. He wondered if she would be able to make a meeting for Wednesday at two, to meet the executives and draw up a project plan. Would she be available on Wednesday?

"Sure, Wednesday sounds good. And I don't mind meeting at your office."

"Sounds good." David recited the address and hung up. Nadia shook her head in exasperation. There was nothing he said that Debbie wouldn't have been able to handle, after confirming the date and time with her, of course. His clients must be really important, she figured, and that was good for business.

In fifteen years, KNG Corporation had grown from medium-sized company to a big one with more than three hundred employees in four countries. The constant advancement in technology and peripheral services had boosted the company's bottom line tremendously, but Nadia knew the growth was more than just that. Employee turnover was one of the lowest in the industry. KNG Corporation's staff was paid very well, from top executives to even the janitor. Excellent benefits and substantial bonuses to deserving employees also contributed to overall satisfaction and loyalty to the company and its mission statement. It hadn't all been roses. There were times she'd wanted to give up and just hand the reins over to Kenneth, but the family wouldn't let her.

The rest of Monday was uneventful. She had lunch with Bettie and Shannon, made some overseas calls, and even had time to catch up on her current reading of Maya Angelou's *I Know Why the Caged Bird Sings*, an autobiography she had been wanting to read for a long time.

By the time she got home in the evening, Emmett had already made dinner: restaurant-bought moo goo gai pan with lots of vegetables, which she really appreciated because she was in no mood to cook. He was just considerate that way, for all of his fifteen years. She knew she was blessed because she saw and read about the struggles single mothers went through all the time.

Sometimes, making enough money was not the issue, but the ability to balance work-life so that the kids were raised right while preserving one's well-being. She didn't have to fret over finding a babysitter or wonder if all her efforts were in vain.

She made sure KNG Corporation's employees had access to subsidized childcare through a special program established by a fund set up in Nick's name. Just like he had been her rock when she needed it, she wanted to make sure that her employees did not need to complain about the inability to get help with their children.

Several scholarships were awarded every year to deserving students and to date fifty college degrees were made possible by full scholarships to study information technology at the University of Houston-Clear Lake. Some of those graduates had even come back to work for KNG Corporation. It was indeed a very successful cycle.

Nadia went all out with her appearance on Wednesday. She had several outfits she referred to as her "power outfits," and it was one of them she chose because of the meeting with David and his clients for later in the day. The skirt suit was pinstripe gray, and she coupled it with a baby pink dress shirt and silver pumps. For power meetings, she liked to be feminine yet give the impression she was no woman to be messed with. Fall for the sweetness at your own peril. She had an early light lunch at Lubby's restaurant, cleared all her morning appointments by eleven, and by twelve was out the door with Kenneth. She let him drive so she could relax and ram up her thoughts on the way.

"I can't wait to see 'the clients,'" Kenneth stated jokingly as they paid for parking in Downtown Houston. Luckily, the building was right across the street, so they didn't have to walk far.

"Business is business," Nadia emphasized. "You never know."

"True, after you." He let her and one other lady enter the elevator before him, and then out of the blue, "Vera and I are having a baby."

"What?" Nadia couldn't believe her ears. "And you choose now to tell me the news? Kenneth!" Nadia couldn't contain her excitement, and the other lady too smiled and congratulated Kenneth. He and Vera had been trying to get pregnant for the past five years. Kenneth had taken his time getting married, and when he met the young attorney at a luncheon five years ago, it was love at second sight. She hadn't liked him initially, and he had to work hard to convince her he was the right guy.

"I'm so happy for you. This calls for a celebration."

"No," Kenneth said. "You are the only one that knows. We don't want to announce it yet." He stopped, suddenly self-conscious that a stranger was also in the elevator with them. "We'll talk about it later."

"OK. It's going to be all right Kenneth."

She held his hand as the elevator made a stop on the ninth floor. So it was, that she was still holding his hand when the doors opened, and Anthony was standing right there. Shock paralyzed her for a second, but she quickly regained her composure and held Kenneth's hand tighter at the narrowed look on his face as he looked at them. They didn't talk to each other. The other elevator soon pinged, and he entered it.

"Do you know him?" Kenneth asked as they looked for the suite number. "He was looking at us weird."

"That's Anthony."

"The Anthony?"

"Yes," she replied succinctly.

"Really?"

"Yes!" she said under her breath. "Can we leave this alone for now? Here's our suite."

The name on the door said Brenner and Associates in gold letters; Nadia was already scoffing at the extravagance, guessing that it was a law firm. Kenneth opened the door. It was a tastefully furnished reception. The secretary was obviously expecting them, and she asked if they wanted coffee or tea before ushering them into a spacious conference room at the end of the sprawling premises.

"I'm Monica, let me know if you need anything. Just push the green button and you can speak with me directly." She pointed to a phone on the desk. "David will be in here shortly."

"Thanks, Monica." Nadia smiled.

"You're welcome." They still had twenty minutes before the meeting started. "Kenneth, really, I can't wait for the baby to arrive. Vera must be thrilled."

"Yes, but we have to be careful. We have been trying for so long that it still seems like a dream, and the doctor advised us to be careful in these first months. In fact, she is on bed rest as we speak. We found out by accident you know. It's very funny. All this while that we had been trying, nothing happened. We actually were supposed to start another round of fertility treatment, went to the doctor, and she asked her to take a pregnancy test in order to run some tests, and voila, the lines were positive!"

"Oh my God, this is unbelievable. Make sure she gets all her rest. You'd have to do a lot of cooking for a while," Nadia joked.

"I don't mind at all." He laughed, then changed the subject. "How about Anthony?"

"What about him?"

"I mean, what are the odds that we'd run into him here? Life is weird sometimes, and you all didn't even talk to each other."

She shrugged. "Beats me, he could have said hi. He wasn't looking very happy seeing us holding hands, I think."

"True. If looks could kill."

"He has no rights whatsoever over me."

"He has Emmett with you," Kenneth interjected softly, just as the door opened and three men walked into the room. David, another white guy, and Anthony.

For all her power readying image, Nadia had no idea how that meeting actually went, but she knew she said the right things and made the right suggestions.

Scott Brenner was a partner in Brenner and Associates. They specialized in estate and oil and gas law. Anthony's law firm was known for litigation, tax, and intellectual property law. Somehow, Anthony had been able to convince the partners that both law firms should merge, the argument was made easier by the fact that he met Scott in law school and they were good friends.

Both companies managed a lot of sensitive data for their clients, hence the need for an upgrade in security for the various software they utilized in their practices. They were also willing to spend as much as it took to do this, which was why they needed the very best. The account was worth millions in the long run. There was a lot of back and forth, arguments and data display, and they emerged from the conference room three hours later with the promise of a proposal and project plan in a week. Kenneth was thrilled. Nadia was thrilled and apprehensive.

"You held yourself well," Kenneth complimented as he drove back to the office so she could get her car. "You did well, Nadia, under the circumstances."

"Don't you think it's not a coincidence? I mean, what are the odds of me bumping into Anthony at the mall and his law firm retaining our services all within a week?" she shook her head. "Methinks something is fishy."

"He still loves you."

"You must be kidding. Kenneth, the last time we had a civil conversation was fifteen years ago. He got married, had two children, and you think he still has the hots for me? Please be real."

"I'm a man. I can tell. That man still loves you. He couldn't keep his eyes off you, and he was looking at you like he was really proud of you, too."

"How would you know?"

"Everybody could feel the tension, Nadia. It was there, subtle yet powerful, between you two. You tried so hard not to show it, but we could see it."

"Oh my God." Nadia couldn't believe it. "I don't even feel anything for Anthony anymore, Kenneth."

"He's the father of your son. There's still a bond there," Kenneth pointed out.

"Emmett is Nick's son."

"No, Nadia. Nick stepped in. He would have been, if he was alive. It's been fifteen years, Nadia, and believe me, Emmett is already wondering about his dad, even if he hasn't asked."

"He does know about his biological dad."

"Knowing and meeting are two different things. I suggest you think it over very well, Nadia. Emmett loves you, and the past is the past. Don't let it get to a stage that he starts resenting you for not initiating a meeting between both of them. The sooner the better," Kenneth suggested, looking at her empathetically. "I do understand how you feel."

"Thanks, Kenneth, I really appreciate it," she said. They were at KNG Corporation premises but were still in the car. "I'm still excited about you and Vera, though. Tell her I'll come visit this weekend. See you tomorrow," Nadia said as she opened the door.

"All right, Nadia, take care. Tell Emmett I said hi."

"Sure. Bye, Kenneth."

CHAPTER SIX

Nadia visited Vera and Kenneth on Saturday, but the rest of the weekend was devoted to Emmett. She liked to do that sometimes so they could catch up on anything they'd missed during the week.

On Sunday, she offered to go to church with him, after which they had lunch at Applebee's. She wanted to use the opportunity to tell him about Anthony, but he beat her to it.

"Mom, I need to talk to you about Dad," he began after dessert. "I—"

"It's OK, Emmett. I was going to say something. When we get home all right?"

"I hope you don't mind, Mom," he continued in the car.

"Oh no, not at all. It was bound to come up sooner or later."

He was quiet after that, preoccupied with his thoughts, and she let him be. At home, she told him how she had bumped into Anthony and the meeting with Brenner and Associates.

"It's definitely not a coincidence," he stated when she was done. "You think maybe he's looking for a way to get back with you? I mean, he's divorced…" His voice trailed off.

"Maybe, maybe not. Whatever it may be, I have to find a way to connect you two."

"Won't he be mad that you didn't tell him sooner?"

"Why should he be mad? Remember, he's the one who pulled a disappearing act. If I'd let him know after he was married, I would be labeled a home-wrecker."

"True, but I really appreciate your honesty with me, Mom." He kissed her on the cheek. "You're the best mom ever."

Nadia laughed. "Thanks, son, I know you can't wait to meet your dad."

"Yes and no. I'm excited but also nervous. He has children, and I can't expect him to just have a bond with me overnight."

"Wise words, but Anthony is a reasonable man, in spite of everything. I'm sure all will be all right. Don't worry too much about it, OK?"

"Yes, Mom."

Nadia sighed as she watched Emmett go. She didn't know much about Anthony's present life except what she heard from Lizzy. As much as she didn't want anything to do with him, she knew she had to put aside her feelings for Emmett's sake.

On Monday, she asked Kenneth to start working on the proposal so it could be ready as early as possible. She also told him about her talk with Emmett and her decision to tell Anthony the truth.

"It's the best under the circumstances," Kenneth said as he gave her a light hug.

"Yes." Nadia let herself be comforted. "Thanks so much. You and the family have been so good to me."

"What's not to like about you, Nadia? You're—"

He was interrupted by Anthony's presence as he came in the door.

"Hi, Anthony. What a surprise! We weren't expecting you." Nadia was happy Kenneth hadn't released her immediately. She didn't want Anthony to start thinking that he had any rights whatsoever where she was concerned. And he hadn't called that he was coming.

If Anthony felt anything at seeing them in a hug, he didn't show it.

"I know, I had to come see you guys because I'm traveling on Wednesday evening, and I don't know how quickly that proposal can be ready."

"That shouldn't be a problem. We promised a week, so it should be on your desk by noon. You could just have called though, instead of showing up here unannounced." Nadia went to sit behind her desk. "I'll work with Kenneth myself to make sure it's ready," she said coolly.

She really didn't appreciate the way he just walked into her office like he owned it, even if he looked the part in his sharp three-piece and expensive Windsor's suit.

"I'll talk to you later, Nadia," Kenneth said as he left.

"All right, Kenneth," Nadia said. She felt bereft of support, but she was ready for this. "Yes, Anthony."

"Hi," he began, shutting the door behind Kenneth.

"Please leave my door alone," she said stiltedly.

"I need to talk to you in private, Nadia." He shut it anyway and came to sit opposite her. "We need to get along."

She twirled a pencil in her hand. "Obviously."

"Nadia, we need to be civil if we're going to be working together," he reminded her. "Let the past be the past, OK?"

"It's easy for you to say, Anthony, but this is not the time and place for this conversation. Besides, we were civil in the last meeting."

"I know. I'm sorry, OK? I had to come see you." He looked around the office. "You've done well for yourself. I've known about KNG Corporation for years especially after the owner died fifteen years ago. What a tragic loss. I also heard that his wife took over the reins…" His voice trailed off. "Wait…Gardner!" He stood up suddenly. "You were married to him?" he asked incredulously.

"Yes."

"Oh my God, Nadia. It didn't take long for you to find another warm body for your bed I see. Wow"

He was cut short by a resounding slap on his face.

He gazed at her in astonishment.

Nadia was breathing heavily, unable to contain her fury. "Don't you ever, ever, come into my office and insult me, Anthony. You are the one who went MIA!"

He seized her arms, his nostrils flaring. "And don't you ever, ever, lay your hands on me again, Nadia," he hissed.

She winced at his hold, making him step back immediately.

"God, you have the worst effect on me. I didn't mean to do that, OK? Please don't go telling your boyfriend anything."

"Kenneth is not my boyfriend. He is my brother-in-law, you buffoon!"

If anything, the name-calling only made him laugh. "God, Nadia. It's OK. I'm sorry. Buffoon? Who uses that word these days? Look." He offered a hand. "Truce? I came here with sincere intentions, trust me. This is exactly what I was trying to prevent, us going at each other rehashing the past when there are companies' reputations and lots of money on the line."

She took the offer. The contact sent warmth through her. "We start afresh." She went behind her desk. "How are your girls?"

"They're good…being teenagers as usual, at least one. Erin is thirteen, and Yazmine is eleven but thinks she's fifteen. How about your child? Weren't you pregnant at the time of Nick's death?" His voice had softened. "I'm really sorry, Nadia. Never in a million years would I have thought—"

"It's been fifteen years. Good memory. My son is fine." She looked him straight in the eye. "There's something I need to tell you, Anthony, but not here in the office. We have to meet somewhere."

"What is it? Sounds important."

"It is. But not here like this."

"Give me a hint," he pressed.

"It's about my son."

"Your son?"

"Yes, Emmett."

"What about him?"

"He is your son, Anthony," she replied.

His jaw dropped. He stared at her for a long time. "So, you were pregnant with him when you married Nick?"

"Yes."

"Oh my God! Nadia, why didn't you say something?"

She shrugged, looking at him levelly. "For obvious reasons. And I called. Multiple times. You didn't return any calls. I knew I wasn't dialing the wrong number, so obviously, you didn't want to pick my calls. Look, Anthony, that's why I told you it's something we have to discuss in private. Let's meet after you come back from your trip, OK?"

He didn't argue. "Does he know about me?"

"He's always known about you, and he can't wait to meet you."

"Wow, Nadia, I really messed up, didn't I?" he came to stand by her. "Forgive me?"

She stood up, feeling overpowered by his nearness. She caught a faint scent of familiar cologne.

"We'll talk when you get back," she said firmly. "I have a business to run."

"Yes." On impulse, he kissed her on the forehead. "Thank you."

"For what?"

"I've always wanted a son."

Nadia didn't respond to that.

He walked toward the door. "I should be back by Sunday night. I'll call you as soon as I can so we can meet."

"All right. That proposal will definitely be on your desk by noon on Wednesday."

He looked back. "I trust you, Nadia. Just to let you know, I am very proud of you."

"Thanks."

He opened the door and left.

Nadia sank back into the welcoming comfort of her chair. Her relationship with Anthony always seemed to be in a whirlwind. She needed to strategize so she didn't get caught up in whatever he was brewing. In a way, she knew Anthony. And in a way, she didn't really know him at all. She just knew the business arrangement they had going on, though lucrative for KNG Corporation, was not a coincidence. She needed to keep things strictly business, even while discussing Emmett with him.

True to her words, the proposal was delivered to David on Wednesday morning. Nadia's mind was in turmoil, though. She told Emmett about the incident in her office, He seemed to take it calmly, but she was worried about the ripple effects of a meeting with his dad. Emmett was a very level-headed young man, but he was still a kid and she didn't want the current situation to affect his academic and athletic performances at school, especially as he was doing so well and on the way to getting a football scholarship in his senior year. There were also Erin and Yazmine to consider. They definitely were not so young that they wouldn't understand the implication of having a brother thrust on them at these stages of their lives when the divorce between their parents was still so fresh.

Nadia retired to bed early on Sunday night, determined to get at least half of *I Know Why the Caged Bird Sings* read by nine. Anthony still had not called, and she steeled herself against worrying about his well-being. Nick's untimely death had made her value life and relationships more. Life could be so fleeting, and people got carried away with the busyness that they often forget what was more important. She shouldn't be worrying about Anthony at all, but there was nothing bad in being concerned for his well-being.

The phone rang promptly at nine, just as she was putting the book away, jarring her thoughts. It was Anthony.

"Hey."

"Hi."

"I just got back into town." He sounded really tired. "I'm still at the airport waiting for my taxi as we speak. Can we meet tomorrow at my place?"

"I don't think that's a good idea," Nadia replied. "Your daughters—"

"They'll be in school, Nadia, and I don't think I'll go to the office, either. I like to take a day off after this kind of travel to refresh."

"OK," she capitulated. "Give me the address."

He recited his address to her. "All right. How have you been? And Emmett?"

"We're good. See you tomorrow, Anthony. Go get some rest, OK?"

"Yeah, thanks. See you then." He hung up.

Nadia would have preferred they met on neutral ground, but she was a reasonable woman. She could have rescheduled anyway but wanted to get it out of the way as soon as possible so everybody could move on with their lives.

Anthony lived in a new subdivision in Richmond, Texas. She drove to his address without effort. It was a really nice house with well-kept gardens and fountain in the front yard. She knocked on the door.

He opened the door in his robe. "Hi, Nadia. Come in," he greeted.

"Morning." She smiled, pleasantly surprised at the warmth of the living room. She purposely avoided the couch and sat on a chair instead, looking around. "Very nice."

"Thanks, and in case you're wondering, I decorated it myself."

"You?" she asked in disbelief. "I didn't know you had it in you."

"I've picked up quite a few skills over the past couple of years." He shrugged. "You want coffee? Tea?"

"Do you have orange juice?"

"You bet. Be right back."

Nadia couldn't help noticing his strong legs as he walked into the kitchen. "Who takes care of the girls?"

"I have a nanny, but I gave her the day off since you were coming. Privacy," he answered as he walked back with a glass. He handed it to her.

"Liz told me about the divorce."

For a second, she thought she caught a faint glimpse of pain in his eyes. "It's one of those things. She wanted it."

"So, you wouldn't have divorced her despite the affair?"

"I really wanted my kids to grow up with both parents, but it would have been a death sentence to keeping living with Sara under the circumstances. It's not a joyful thought to wonder about whom your wife has slept with during the day when you're making love to her at night. I had to let go."

"Hmm."

"You look nice," he said out of the blue. "And you looked so sexy in your suit at the meeting, too."

"Please, Anthony, don't start."

"But it's true. How did you meet Nick?"

"At work. He was a customer at the gas station."

"So, he married you despite your being pregnant by another man?"

Nadia shook his head. "Let's not go there, Anthony. You are not in any position to pass judgments, really."

"I just wondered."

"He loved me, so don't go thinking otherwise," She added. "And we're here to talk about your son, not Nick."

"True. You should have told me, though. I would have taken care of my responsibility."

"Wow! Anthony, listen to yourself. I called you a million times. You never returned my calls. Obviously, it was just a booty call for you, right? And you said you loved me, didn't you? Maybe if you had picked my calls before you went to Nigeria to get married. And how would your wife have felt? It's easier said than done."

"We would have found a way," he maintained.

"You are a man, so you wouldn't understand. Anyway, Emmett can't wait to see you."

"I wonder how he'll feel."

"Depends on you, Anthony. I would suggest you don't force it, let the bond develop naturally."

"I did some research. He's quite the football player."

Nadia's face lit up with pride. "He's really good. I see scholarships in his future."

"Not that he needs it, though, I've also done my research on KNG Corporation. You are a very generous leader, Nadia,"

"I've got to keep the people happy. We at the top just make decisions, but the nitty gritty of a company's success is seventy-five percent mid- to entry-level employees' effort."

"Who cannot function without the decisions of the big executives?" Anthony countered. "Both are equally important."

"True." Nadia looked at her watch. "I have a meeting at one, so I won't be staying long."

Anthony smiled. "And here I was, thinking we would spend the day together."

"Are you serious? For what? I know you're joking, Anthony."

"Why didn't you ever remarry?"

"It's none of your business."

"You'd have to someday you know. You can't be alone forever."

"When I meet the right person, then I'll cross that bridge." Her voice was cool.

"I'm only looking out for you, Nadia. Please don't take offense."

She laughed in incredulity. "You are a piece of work, Anthony. What right do you have after what you did to me to even make any kind of assumption or believe that I'd trust your concern for my well-being?"

"I do care about you."

"Wow! Really!" She stood up. "I've got to go. I'll call you and figure out when you and Emmett can meet. He has a football game this weekend out of town, so it'll have to be the following week."

"Where is the game? Maybe I can come along."

"No…don't think that's a good idea. After you guys meet, all that can be ironed out. Besides, have you thought about your girls' feelings in all this?"

"He is their brother."

"Who they're meeting for the first time. It's going to be a big shock you know."

"Erin and Yazmine will adapt very well. I mean, they were devastated by the divorce but doing really well now."

"This is different. They might see Emmett as competing for your love and affection, including the time they now have to split with him."

"I see your point of view," Anthony agreed. "Do you think I should tell them?"

"That would be a good idea."

"I'll see what I can do."

"Yes," Nadia was standing by the door. He came to stand by her. "I'll see you later."

"Nadia." He suddenly pulled her toward him, burying his face in her hair. "I've missed you."

"Anthony, let go." Nadia struggled to free herself. "This is not appropriate."

"What?" He released her slowly. "We're two consenting adults."

"We're not in a relationship."

"Give me a break, Nadia. We don't have to be in a relationship for me to hug you, OK? After all, I see you and Kenneth hugging all the time. One would think you were lovers."

"No comment to that."

He opened the door for her. His eyes were devoid of expression. "I'll see you soon."

"Right," Nadia said as she walked to her car, her agitation at what his nearness had awakened in her artfully concealed. "Bye."

"Bye, Nadia." He stood, watching, as she started the car and drove off.

Nadia was a ball of nerves as she drove. She couldn't believe how cool she'd been throughout their conversation. Their frequent meetings were beginning to resurrect long-buried feelings, emotions she really couldn't afford to deal with at the moment. If at all, not with Anthony. She would be very foolish to easily forget what happened between them and the callous way he had abandoned her in the past. Twice to be exact: first, when she arrived in Texas from Pennsylvania on his invitation, and second when he left her to go marry somebody else from Nigeria. Those memories still evoked some pain in her no matter how she tried to forestall them.

One thing she wouldn't do was begrudge the relationship she must now foster between Anthony and Emmett. Certainly, there would be many obstacles to tackle along the way. She just hoped and prayed that whatever bumps they encountered would only cement cordiality and not strife.

Emmett's school won the game on Saturday, fifteen-seven. Nadia went with Kenneth and Lorraine, and she was quite the proud mother as she watched Emmett score two touchdowns for his team. Kenneth drove and it was midnight by the time they got back to Houston. As Emmett took off his shoes and put them up in the in the mudroom, Nadia watched him with keen eyes. He had been subdued on the way home.

"Is everything OK?"

"Yes, Mom," he replied, but his voice was shaky.

She approached him cautiously, for he was at that stage where hugging was an anathema to him sometimes. "What is it, Emmett?"

"I wish Dad was there today," he said quietly.

"Oh, Emmett!" She hugged him, and he didn't protest. "He wanted to, but I felt you two should meet first. There'll be plenty of times, Emmett."

"I know." He stepped away from her. "I've got to go take a shower. I'm tired."

Nadia left him alone, her heart contracting with love as he walked up the stairs. Her phone rang. "Hi, Anthony."

"Hi. Are you guys all right? Just checking on you, make sure you're back safe."

"We just got back," Nadia volunteered. "His team won, fifteen-seven. He scored two touchdowns."

"Wow! That's my boy. I can't wait to see him, Nadia. How is he?"

"He's fine. Went up to take a shower and probably sleep. I didn't play any game, and I'm tired myself."

"Did you drive?"

"Kenneth did, one of Kenneth's aunts went with us, too. It was fun." She laughed, releasing some stress.

"That's good. All right then, I just called to make sure you guys are good. We'll talk later."

"Sure, thanks," Nadia said. "How are the girls?"

"At their mother's this weekend. I have the house all to myself. Even the nanny is off." He dropped his voice. "I'm the only one here."

"Oh no, Anthony, it's not going to happen." She caught on to his banter immediately. "In your dreams."

"Hmm…never say never."

"Hmm…never," Nadia joked, laughing. "Thanks for checking on us. OK, got to go now."

"All right. Bye."

After he hung up Nadia stood for several minutes, pondering. It was certainly thoughtful of him to call, but she was wary of his true intentions even amidst all the jokes.

"Oh, well," she sighed, suddenly feeling deflated.

Slowly, she went upstairs to her room, knocking on Emmett's door on the way. He didn't answer, so she peeped in. He was fast asleep. On a whim, she tiptoed to his bed and gave him a kiss on the forehead.

Just as she was about to leave, his phone started ringing. Nadia knew better, but she looked anyway. It was a girl. She smiled. Her little boy was growing up fast. She felt no fear because they had had many conversations regarding that topic, and she trusted him to be responsible in his relationships with the fairer sex.

Sunday was a lazy day. She stayed in bed until ten, didn't come downstairs till twelve, ate some leftovers, and went right back up to catch up on bills and finish her reading. Nadia was content and happy as she tinkered around the house later in the evening, making dinner and have another subtle "conversation" with Emmett about relationships.

He shook his head. "Mom, you know me better than that. I'm not stupid."

"I know, son, but mistakes happen. Don't go dabbling in grown folk business until you're ready for grown folk responsibility."

"Leave it alone, Mom. I don't even have a girlfriend yet. I'm fifteen for God's sake."

"You better remember that." she stressed, jokingly. They did this occasionally, and Emmett knew his mother was just being protective, as any mother would be.

"I'm not dating till I'm eighteen," he vowed.

"Geez, don't go overboard, son," Nadia chided. "Just be careful, OK?"

"All right." He stood up from the barstool to plant a kiss on her cheek. "I love you, Mom."

"Love you too, son."

After dinner, Nadia decided to pamper herself with a bath, and she went all out. Thirty lit candles later, she slowly sank into the tub filled with bubbles of her favorite soap, her head wrapped in a towel. She felt thankful as she sat there. She really had nothing to complain about. Once Anthony and Emmett settled in their relationship, maybe she would start going on dates again. She wasn't in a hurry. Life was beautiful.

Anthony called her so frequently that she was starting to think he was behaving like a boyfriend. He invited her to lunch several times, but she declined, unwilling to start anything she couldn't finish. She felt little sparks during their brief meetings, but that was not enough to sustain a relationship. What was foremost on her mind now was Emmett and the girls' well-being. She wondered if Anthony was trying to kill two birds with one stone and snag her in the process of reconciling with Emmett.

So, when he showed up in her office on Thursday, she wasn't surprised. He strolled in, looking handsome and confident in blue checkered shirt and dark gray slacks. She was sitting behind her desk wondering where to go for lunch.

"You don't give up, do you?"

"Not good for business." He sat down. "You refuse to take my calls. And your secretary lied to me that you were in a long meeting that will last all day. I'm beginning to think you got a secretary just to keep me at bay," he accused.

"Believe me, you're not that important," she said with a straight face. "You can't just keep coming into my office like you own or run the place, Anthony. Courtesy, courtesy."

"Ouch, that hits below the belt." He held his abdomen jokingly.

"Why did she let you in?" Nadia said in reproof of the secretary. He obviously didn't take her words seriously.

"Please go easy on her. She had no choice against my charm."

She raised her brows. "Really? I don't see anything but a man intent on disrupting my work."

"You know that's not true. I've come to take you out to lunch."

"Already had lunch."

"Liar." He laughed. "That's one lie your secretary didn't tell. How can you have had lunch? It's just eleven thirty."

"I brought my lunch," she insisted.

"Come on, Nadia. I know a very good Chinese place downtown."

"Not in the mood for Chinese food."

"Please." He stood up. "I promise you the fried rice is out of this world. If it's not so, I promise never to ever, ever, bother you for lunch again."

"Promise?"

"Scout's honor. Deal?"

She laughed. "Deal."

They left the office, Nadia pretending not to notice the curious looks they elicited from employees. She cared about her employees, but her personal business was hers alone. Besides, she couldn't be hostile to Anthony just because. He was Emmett's dad.

And he was right. The fried rice was indeed the best she'd ever eaten, so much so that she got two orders to go. It was a surprisingly good meal, and they found a lot to talk about during the two hours they were together.

"We should do this more often."

"You mean, invading my office and dragging me to lunch? Naaaa."

Anthony laughed. "It was nice, though. Admit it, Nadia."

"True, I like your company. But we shouldn't make a habit of this, or people will start thinking something is happening between us."

"Would that be so bad?"

"Not really, but I am not ready for a relationship now. My focus is on Emmett and the relationship between you two."

They were almost at KNG Corporation's premises. He pulled into the parking lot of an adjacent building and killed the engine of the Mercedes.

"Why are you parking here?" Nadia asked. "You know I have a meeting in an hour, and I need to go prepare my papers."

"Nadia, I just want you to keep an open mind about us, OK?" he began. "I'm not saying you should jump into a relationship with, me, but don't let a good thing pass you by, either."

She scoffed. "A good thing? I thought I had a good thing fifteen years ago, and look where it landed me, pregnant and alone. Look, Anthony, please take me back to work. I'm not angry with you or anything. I just don't think a relationship with you is a wise decision. I've got too much going on."

"You can't be alone forever, Nadia," he stated quietly. "I'll be here whenever you're ready."

"What you should be concerned with is Emmett."

"I am concerned about Emmett. Bring him by this weekend so we can meet." He started the car. "Sara has the girls again. They have a birthday party, and she volunteered to take them."

"That won't be a problem. We'll be there at eleven."

"Good." A few minutes later he was back at KNG Corporation. "See you then."

"Yes, thanks for lunch."

"You're welcome," he said coolly and drove off.

Nadia could feel the buzz as soon as she entered the building. Even the receptionist in the lobby had a strange smile on her face. Nadia shook her head as she got on the elevator. Kenneth was waiting for her in the office.

"Hmm…I'm jealous," he joked. "Why wasn't I invited to lunch?"

"'Cos three is a crowd." Nadia placed a bag on the desk and brought out a square Styrofoam plate. "I brought something back for you. The fried rice is really good."

"Don't change the subject, Nadia," Kenneth said, suddenly sounding serious. "I hope you know what you're doing, I don't want you to get hurt."

"I'm good, Kenneth, it was just a friendly lunch, OK? Thanks for the concern."

He shrugged. "If you say so. The three o' clock meeting was canceled. Last-minute trip. We rescheduled it for next month."

"Isn't that too far off?" This particular client had been complaining that KNG Corporation should give them a hefty discount since they were bringing another partner into the account. "Why were they bothering us then? I don't understand people sometimes."

"Beats me. Got to go. Vera sends her greetings. Just be careful with Anthony, OK? You know he's also a client."

"Yes, thanks, Kenneth," Nadia said as she turned her desktop computer on. "I'll keep that in mind."

It was easier said than done, though. Anthony was in her thoughts a lot. Every time they got together her feelings grew. Indeed, if not for past sins she could easily fall for Anthony all over again. He treated her well, was ever the gentleman, and called or texted to check on her. And she felt that Lizzy was in on it too because she always managed to bring him into the conversation whenever she called now, dropping hints and making subtle suggestions about Nadia's single status.

Anthony called just as she was about to leave the office. "Hi."

"Hey. I was just leaving."

"OK. Would it be OK to you bring Emmett by at two instead of eleven on Saturday? There is some last-minute tidying up I need to do for a client, so I'm meeting him in the morning, but I should be back home by twelve."

"That's fine."

"Good. And have you given a thought to what I said?"

"What is that?"

"About you being my girl."

Nadia was quiet. His words brought back memories from when they first met in Nigeria. Emotions welled in her. "Anthony, you know it's not going to work."

"Why? I still love you, Nadia."

"Really? You were married to somebody else for fifteen years, Anthony."

"But I still love you."

"I'm a big girl, Anthony, and would very much appreciate the truth. How could you love me when you dumped me like hot water? Do you even pay attention to your words sometimes?" She was angry. "I would be really, really disappointed if you took me for a fool, talking about you've always loved me."

"But it's the truth. There's a reason for what happened between us, just so you know."

"Really? You were forced to marry that woman?"

"Let's leave it alone. It's complicated. But I did love and still love you. I know you don't believe that."

"You're darn right I don't!" Nadia yelled. "Actions speak louder than words!"

"Calm down, OK? I do understand your point of view. I would feel the same in your shoes. Anyway, like I said, you and Emmett can come by around two. Would you like anything special prepared for you?"

"Don't go to the trouble."

"What about Emmett? What's his favorite food? Drink? Snacks?"

"Why don't you ask him yourself? That's the purpose of the meeting, isn't it?"

"Very well. See you then."

"Bye."

"Bye!" The nerve! She fumed as she got her purse. "Men!"

CHAPTER SEVEN

"Nervous?" Nadia asked Emmett just before she rang the doorbell. She noticed the uncanny resemblance to Anthony at that moment as Emmett stood sharply dressed in a polo shirt and jeans. His hands were in his pockets.

He smiled. "Who wouldn't be, Mom? I've rehearsed this day over and over and I still feel—"

He stopped short as the door opened, and Anthony stood before them. Just for a moment. Before he enclosed his son in a bear hug. Nadia watched as emotions welled in her. She never thought he would be so affected. Both had tears running down their faces when they finally let go a few minutes later.

"Hi, son." Anthony shook Emmett's hand. "Wow!" He was clearly speechless.

"Hi, Dad." Emmett tried to smile, but his voice was hoarse from all the emotions welling up inside him.

"Let's go inside, guys," Nadia suggested.

The initial meeting had gone better than she anticipated. She followed them inside the house and sat for an hour as they talked as if they'd known each other for years. Anthony was undoubtedly impressed by Emmett. Anytime he said something he thought was amazing he would turn to her and nod as if acknowledging her for a job well done. Especially when Emmett revealed that he read Mario Puzo's *Godfather* from cover to cover in fifth grade.

"Anyone care for a drink?" Nadia said after a while. "I'm thirsty!"

"Sorry, I got carried away." Anthony laughed as he stood up. "Come on, son."

Emmett followed his father like they had been doing the same thing for years. Nadia was stunned. She couldn't believe the ease with which they'd taken to each other. That was one thing she admired about guys in general. They didn't let anything cloud the big picture when it came what mattered most. They soon came back with drinks, and Emmett handed her a glass of orange juice.

"Is that OK?"

"Yes. Thanks, Emmett."

Emmett finally had time to look around the room and noticed the pictures of Erin and Yazmine on the mantelpiece. He walked over to examine them closely. "Are these my sisters?"

"Yes," Anthony said behind him. "Erin is the one in blue jeans. She's thirteen. Yazmine is eleven."

"Wow…I have sisters…awesome." He turned to Anthony. "How often does a guy get a father and sisters just like that? Do they know about me?"

"Not yet. I'll have to tell them this week. Wanted to meet you first and let them know what kind of brother they're getting," Anthony said jokingly, patting Emmett on the shoulder. "You're a very good boy."

"I owe it all to Mom," Emmett stated.

"Yes, she's awesome, isn't she?" Anthony said, and they both turned to look at her.

Nadia smiled as she threw a hand up in mock modesty. "Guys, please stop. Is there anything in this house to eat? I'm famished!"

"I'm not that bad, Nadia," Anthony said. "Give me fifteen minutes." He disappeared into the kitchen.

"Would you believe I cooked this myself?" Anthony said as they sat down to eat later, a meal of baked salmon laden with tartar sauce, asparagus, and mini baked potatoes.

"You? Cook?" Nadia asked skeptically. "You couldn't even boil an egg!"

"Had to learn for the girls," he replied. "What kind of father would I be if I can't even make a toast?"

"Well, well, well." Nadia nodded in approval. "You were finally domesticated I see."

"Not exactly so." He smiled. "I make a mean egg sandwich, too."

"Do they eat African food?" Emmett asked. "Wow…this is good, Dad…Mom couldn't have done it better."

"Wow…you've only known your dad for hours, and you're already comparing us. How soon betrayal is wrought."

"Oh no, Mom, you're still the best," Emmett corrected.

Anthony laughed. "Don't be scared, Nadia. To answer your question, the girls do eat some African food. Fried plantains, sweet bread, pounded yam with spinach—"

"They eat pounded yam?"

"Yes, in fact that's Erin's favorite. With her fingers too, like we do back home."

"That's good. Mom makes that for me sometimes. I like it with okra. I hope to visit Africa someday."

"We're planning to go after he graduates from high school," Nadia chipped in.

"I can take him with me next summer. I'm planning to go with the girls," Anthony volunteered.

"I would love to!" Emmett said excitedly.

"We'll see," Nadia said. She loved the way both were getting along but wanted to be cautious. Who knew what the next week would bring? She didn't want Emmett to get his hopes up too high.

They were finally ready to leave at seven in the evening. Nadia held back as Emmett walked to the car. "That went smoother than I thought."

"You've done a good job, Nadia. I couldn't have done better myself. He truly is a remarkable young man," Anthony observed. "Very respectful and calm, too."

"He has some really good models. It was a joint effort with Nick's family. They really supported me."

"I need to meet them sometime."

"We'll see," Nadia said.

He turned to her. "Thank you."

"He's my son too, Anthony."

"Yeah, I know. Thank you all the same." He kissed her lightly on the lips.

She didn't begrudge him that. He followed her to the car and opened the door. "Corvette. Hmm."

"It was Nick's. And, yes, I love driving it."

"Nothing wrong with that." He kissed her again.

Nadia couldn't talk because Emmett was watching them, but she was sure Anthony saw the reprimand in her eyes. "Bye."

"Bye, Emmett," Anthony waved as they left.

"I really like him. He's a cool guy. I can't wait to meet my sisters. Is it OK if I spend some weekends at his place?"

"Why not? He's your dad, but the matter has to be discussed with the girls. Remember they're younger than you."

"I'm going to be the best big brother ever." Emmett beamed.

"That, I don't doubt one bit," Nadia agreed.

The next several weeks were a whirlwind of activities for Nadia. Lorraine celebrated her sixtieth birthday, the deal with the newly merged Brenner and Okafor, LLC, was finalized, and she had to attend the graduation party for one of KNG Corporation's scholarship recipients, a young Hispanic girl graduating summa cum laude who would be the first person to ever go to college in her family.

She also picked up a Nigerian community magazine at the African store one day and was perusing through when a photo of Anthony and his ex-wife Sara leaped at her. They were sitting together at a chieftaincy party for a prominent Houston doctor. Despite there being about eight other people in the photo, only Anthony and Sara commanded Nadia's attention. Unwillingly, she felt a hint of jealousy.

Questions buzzed around in her mind about their relationship. Anthony had repeatedly told her they remained good friends because of the girls, but those girls could also be the reason for them to rethink their divorce and get back together. She knew she was beginning to develop feelings for him again because he occupied her thoughts half the time. She was curious yet could not bring herself to ask him about it, and he sensed her tension when he called her.

"Is something wrong?"

"No."

"I know you better than that Nadia, you are not a pretender at all so you might as well spill the beans."

"Anthony, I'm fine."

"Suit yourself," he said but was in her office an hour later, uninvited as usual. The secretary had given up on trying to stop him. He stood by her desk. "Nadia, what is it?"

"Nothing. And here you are again, unannounced. I might have to get security to keep you out my office."

"So why the attitude?"

"What attitude?"

"I'm not stupid, Nadia. I can see through you."

"Why are you trying to go out with me if you're still going out with Sara?"

"Sara? Where the heck did you come up with that? The only thing tying Sara and me together are the girls."

"But you went to the chieftaincy party with her."

Anthony laughed. "Oh, that? Are you jealous?"

"No, but I appreciate honesty and integrity in my man."

He stepped nearer to her. She hated having to look up to him. "But I am not your man, Nadia. Have you forgotten how many times you turned me down?"

"Well." She stood up. "I don't mean it that way. But you shouldn't be talking to any other woman about dating her if you have intentions of going back to Sara." His nearness was doing things to her that she couldn't help. She could see the veins in his neck. Smell the cologne he was wearing. Feel his breath on her face. She wanted to get away from the longing gnawing at her, and there was nowhere to go. She could have gone the other side, but she wouldn't give him the satisfaction of knowing what his proximity did to her senses.

"So, what's your concern then?" he asked softly, looking her straight in the eye. "I'm free to date whomever I want, including my ex-wife."

"It's none of my business who you date." The words barely left her lips.

He gave a low, intimate laugh and circled her waist with his arms. "Liar."

"Anthony, no—" Her feeble protests were stopped by a deep and searching kiss she couldn't help participating in. Her senses reeled as he released her slowly. "Are you aware we're in my office?" she whispered, but there was no anger in her voice.

"I lock that door behind me every time for occasions such as this." He smiled. "Feel better?"

"About what? I'm serious, though."

Morayode

"Well, for your information, I have no intention of going back to Sara, ever. The host is a very good friend of ours, and there's no crime in sitting next to her. In fact, if you care to know, the gentleman to her left is her current boyfriend. *Capisce*?"

She shrugged. "You're forgiven."

"There was never any crime to begin with. I'd just appreciate if you asked me about anything instead of jumping to conclusions, OK?"

"Right."

"So, are you saying yes? You'll go out with me?"

"Not really. I have to really think it over, Anthony. Emmett, the girls…"

"They would love you, Nadia."

"I'll think about it, OK? Now get out of here before my staff thinks something else is going on."

Nadia watched him go with mixed feelings. Had she been really jealous of Sara? Should she trust Anthony to be the man he should be this time around? She needed to tread carefully. Anthony had betrayed her twice. She didn't want it to happen a third time, especially now that Emmett was involved. The last thing she needed was a relationship that would disrupt their lives. She maybe could cope, but Emmett. That would be her undoing. She would never ever forgive Anthony if he broke Emmett's heart, never. Her friend felt differently, though.

"Really?" said Lizzy.

Both ladies were sitting at a table on the patio of a popular seafood restaurant near the Galleria in Houston. Lizzy had called that morning, wanting to do lunch, an event they enjoyed at least twice a month in an effort to make girls' time amidst their busy schedules with work and family.

"You know what I think already. You should go for it, Nadia. Anthony's a good man."

"Oh, how soon we forget," Nadia chided. "You were right there when it all happened."

"Fifteen years ago. You've got to let the past go, Nadia," Lizzy reminded. She started singing the song from Disney's *Frozen*, causing other patrons to smile.

"Don't tell me you know that song?"

"You wouldn't believe what kids will make you do, Nadia."

"Geez! I get it!" Nadia yelled, laughing.

"I am going to go back and get those shoes I saw at Nieman Marcus," said Lizzy. They had been inside the mall earlier. "I love that dark pink color."

"They're marked down too, so it'll be a bargain. You can afford it," Nadia joked.

"Girl, we need to splurge once in a while. I mean, what are we working for? Thank God, we have families who appreciate us."

"True," Nadia concurred. "I used to surprise Nick with something every time I shopped. He loved it."

"It's Anthony's turn," Lizzy quipped.

Nadia raised her brows. "Don't know about that yet."

"So how are the kids getting along? I don't know how I would have managed."

"Surprisingly well, I myself am amazed. Emmett is quite the big brother, and the girls think they are entitled to more spoiling than they already have. Now they have two guys doting on them, I'm envious."

"And pretty soon, it's going to be one big family, happily ever after."

"Ever the optimist, are you?"

"I want you to be happy, Nadia. You deserve it. When Anthony dropped you off at my place fifteen years ago, I never thought our friendship would become so deep. You truly are a good friend, and you know I'm not talking about money." Nadia had given Lizzy a three-bedroom condominium as a graduation present years ago.

"What are friends for? Come on, let's go get those shoes before somebody else buys them."

They spent another two hours window-shopping at the Galleria then parted ways. Nadia was tired, but she believed she got a good workout nonetheless. She stopped by Burger King to get a couple of burgers and went home.

Anthony's Mercedes was in the driveway. He hadn't told her he would be stopping by, and this was one of the reasons she was being cautious. She didn't want any man thinking he could just walk into her life and take over, even if he was Emmett's father.

Anthony and Emmett were in the living room engrossed in a video game. She stood in the doorway watching them for a while, all her irritation melting away. How could she possibly be mad at two guys playing a video game in their downtime?

"Hi, guys!"

They nodded at her. She could see Anthony's appreciation as he turned his head only to briefly scan her simply clad jean-and-turquoise T-shirted frame. She shook her head in exasperation as she dropped the Burger King bags on the island counter in the kitchen. Anthony was supposed to have the girls this weekend. She hoped he hadn't dropped them off at Sara's again just to come spend time with Emmett.

"Anthony," she called. No answer. He had earphones on. She walked to him and shouted in his ear. "Anthony!"

"What! Oh, you made me lose!" he yelled, removing the earphones. "What was that for?"

"I beat you again, Dad!" Emmett said gleefully. "Two to zero!"

"Where are the girls?" Nadia demanded. "Aren't you supposed to have them this weekend?"

"They're with Sara."

"Again? What excuse did you give this time?"

"Simmer down, Nadia. Their mom took them to a birthday party, OK?"

"Good enough." She turned. "I don't want them to start feeling booted out of daddy time."

Anthony looked at Emmett. Both of them smiled. "Mother hen," Anthony joked.

"Whatever. I bought burgers. Didn't know you'd be here, but today is your lucky day. Emmett usually eats two burgers so you can have one of his," she told Anthony.

"I can eat something else."

He followed her into the kitchen where she was opening the fridge. He was right behind her, and she bumped into him as she straightened.

"Always running into me woman," he said quietly, casting a glance at Emmett. He gave her a swift kiss. "You look so sexy in those jeans."

"Emmett!" she whispered.

He laughed. "He is a big boy, Nadia." He bit a chunk off a Whopper. "Hmm…heaven."

"You're incorrigible. Come on, Emmett, the food is getting cold."

They ate in companionable silence for some minutes, then Emmett excused himself. "Got to go get my things ready for school, and my room's a mess. See you later, Dad."

"A'right, son. I'll try to make it to your home game on Wednesday."

"All right. I'll be the most handsome guy on the field," he joked.

"Get ahold of yourself, Emmett, but don't worry, I'll pay close attention to number twenty."

"You shouldn't come here unannounced, Anthony," Nadia said as soon as Emmett was out of earshot. "I understand you wanting to spend time with him, but please let me know beforehand."

"Does he have to get permission to invite his friends over, too?"

"He's just fifteen, Anthony. Remember he's a teenager. You have to pay close attention or else."

"But Emmett is a good boy. Don't be so overprotective, Nadia."

"Please, don't come into my house and tell me how to raise my son, which I've been doing alone for fifteen years."

"Please lower your voice," Anthony scolded. "We don't want him worrying about us now, do we?"

"It's only common courtesy that I would really appreciate, OK? After all, this is my house. I don't want to tell him to ask me for permission because you know…" She shrugged. "I want everything to be open and smooth. You be the bigger man and call or text me to let me know. That's all I ask."

He nodded. "Fair enough. You're so delightful when you're angry."

"Flattery won't get you anywhere, Anthony."

"I would never do such a thing!" He crossed his arms over his chest. He had on a T-shirt that stretched as he did that, showing the muscles under the light fabric.

Her heart skipped a beat. "I need to start making dinner, since I don't think those burgers filled you guys any" she said, flustered.

"Nadia, you know I still love you, right?"

"Anthony—"

"Look, just give me a chance, please? I admit I wronged you, I apologize for not being there for you and Emmett, so let me make it up to both of you."

"You've already more than done that. Games, rides, being there for him. What more?"

"What about you?" he asked softly. "I want to be there for you, Nadia. Let's get married and raise these kids together."

"Are you proposing to me?"

"How else am I going to get you in my bed?"

"Anthony! What if Emmett hears you?"

"He's upstairs in his room. So, what's your answer?"

She fanned herself with her hands. "This is too much too soon."

"I'm not in a hurry. And stop looking like the world's about to turn upside down."

She managed a smile. "Literally, yes. Didn't you say you could cook?"

"Huh, what about that?"

"How about you cook us dinner? Let's see your potential first-hand," she teased. "It might help push your application forward in the decision process." In a way, Nadia was getting tired of constantly trying to ward him off. She was a big girl, and she could handle Anthony and any intentions he might have.

"I'm good, in other areas too, you know."

"Don't even start. Emmett could come back down any minute, and you have no shame whatsoever. So, what you gonna make?"

"Depends on what you have available." He started rummaging through the pantry and cabinets, and she smiled. She might just get used to this.

True to his words, Anthony whipped up a superbly cooked honey mustard grilled chicken with sautéed mushrooms, beans, and slightly fried rice with bean sprouts. Dinner was a light-hearted and pleasant affair; Emmett soon went upstairs again after eating, and Nadia was beginning to get suspicious of his disappearing acts, leaving them alone in the living room. She mentioned this to Anthony.

"He's a smart kid. What do you expect? He wants his parents to be together."

She eyed him. "Are you sure you didn't put him up to anything?"

"Nope." He stood up abruptly. "I've got to get going, I really enjoyed myself today, Nadia."

"Which part? The video games, the burgers? The food?"

"This, I enjoyed the most." He kissed her slowly. "And I want more."

"I know, but have you heard the one about good things coming to those who wait?" She tapped his chest playfully. "Off you go, Mr. Okafor."

"Yeah. Bye, Nadia," he said as he headed out the door.

"Bye."

Kenneth was in her office promptly on Monday. He perched himself on the edge of her desk. "Hmm...I've been hearing stories," he began.

She pretended not to catch his drift. "About what?"

"About one Anthony being a frequent visitor at the house."

"He proposed to me, Kenneth. I just don't know what to do."

"Marry him, Nadia. He seems like a nice guy. And I checked him out, too."

"You did?"

"Yes, I wouldn't have anybody just walk off the streets and come proclaim some great love they don't feel for my favorite girl. You deserve a lot more."

"He is so good with Emmett."

"Yeah, and that boy loves his dad, too. I can feel it every time we talk. What's actually holding you back?"

"History…he certainly doesn't have the best track record with me," she explained.

"He was young then. Just marry the man, and put him out of his misery, OK? But to be serious, I think he means well. You know I wouldn't sanction anything that would cause you harm, Nadia…you and Emmett. And the devil you know is better than the angel you don't know."

"Kenneth, believe me when I say I do have feelings for the man, but Anthony's track record is a bust where I'm concerned. How is Vera?" she subtly changed the subject to his favorite topic. "Off bed rest?"

"Yes. Doing better than expected. It's as if both of us are pregnant, but it's a nice experience, though."

"Try carrying a baby in your belly for nine months. That's the real deal right there. Still, don't let her overwork herself. Easy on her feet, too."

"Right, well, I just came in to check on you. You want to go to lunch later?"

"I'll pass, brought my own sammich. BLT. There's an extra if you want."

"Naaa, I skipped breakfast, so it's got to be hearty. I'm in the mood for some seriously good fried chicken and Cajun rice. Bring you some?"

"No, but thanks. Later."

"All right. And give our discussion a thought. The sooner the better."

"OK, brother."

"Haha."

Anthony called later that night and they talked for almost an hour before Nadia went to bed. However, uncharacteristic of him, there was no call on Tuesday. On Wednesday, she expected, at least, a text to confirm if he would be attending Emmett's game and started getting worried when Emmett told her he had been trying to call him on Tuesday, but he wasn't picking up his calls. She did not want to panic or make any assumptions, especially in front of Emmett. When she called Anthony's phone it went straight to voicemail. She didn't want to call David for fear of creating any suspicion, but she was beginning to get worried.

By the time they got back from the game on Wednesday, Nadia had reached her boiling point. How could Anthony have stood his own son up like that without as much as a phone call? She felt sorry for Emmett as he slowly headed upstairs looking dejected. He tried not to show it, but she knew he was fighting back tears. She almost cried herself for being so foolish to think that Anthony had changed. How could he do this to her a third time? This was so unfair. Lizzy might have news about him, but she wasn't in the mood for a pity party, either.

She thought she would explode with the pain inside of her at the thought that not only her heart but Emmett's was being ripped apart by Anthony's callous behavior. She skipped her usual therapeutic bath for a shower as her anger almost spilled over. The phone rang just as she was toweling dry. It was David.

"Nadia," he began.

"Yes." She was sure he could feel the fury in her voice.

"Anthony asked me to call you."

"Yes?"

"He's in the hospital. He's been there for the past three days."

"What?" she shouted, so loud that Emmett came knocking on the door.

"Are you OK, Mom?"

"Yes, I'm fine. Go to bed, Emmett. Yes, David? He's been in the hospital for three days, and he's just asking you to call me? Why can't he call himself?"

"He's very sick, Nadia. I can't disclose the details to you but he's at Kelsey-Seybold. You can go see him tomorrow. Visiting hours are already over."

"Visiting hours? How can he be so sick, and we're talking about visiting hours? Is anyone by his side?"

"Yes, his sister, Kate, is there most of the time. And his ex-wife comes and goes, too. But he really wants to see you, OK?"

"All right, all right." She found it hard to come to grips with the news. "I'll go see him tomorrow. Thanks, David."

"You bet. Bye, Nadia."

She decided not to tell Emmett beyond that Anthony had to make an emergency trip at the last minute. She dropped Emmett at school and was at the hospital by eight in the morning. As she took the elevator to the sixth floor her mind was in turmoil. What kind of illness could be so terrible that he had to be hospitalized? Anthony wasn't a fitness enthusiast like Nick, but he took good care of himself and worked out at least twice a week. He even had a treadmill in his office.

She couldn't get Nick out of her mind also. His loss had been very devastating for her, and she was apprehensive to find out what could possibly land Anthony in the hospital.

Room 621 was a private room. Kate was sitting on a chair looking really sad, and Anthony was on the bed hooked to every monitoring gadget imaginable.

Nadia gasped. "Oh my God!" She ran to his bedside, startling Kate.

"Nadia." Her voice was an attempt to be cordial but not friendly.

"Kate. Hi. What happened?"

"You shouldn't be here," Kate snapped.

"What?" Nadia couldn't believe her ears. The lady certainly hadn't grown up! But she wasn't the timid Nadia from years ago. "You haven't changed at all, have you? Why are you so hateful? I got nothing that interests you and nothing of yours interests me, so why the hate?"

"You know you're not good enough for my brother, and you never were," she said so quietly Nadia could barely hear. "Go be with your own kind."

Nadia shook her head in disgust. "I did marry my own kind, Kate. Have you heard of KNG Corporation? In case you don't know, I am the CEO. And that is one heck of a lot more than your kind could ever achieve! Now get out of my way!"

Nadia held Anthony's hand, smirking at the shocked expression on Kate's face. There was a chart by Anthony's bed with the attending nephrologist's name on it. Nadia went to look for Dr. Livingston. He looked to be in his mid-forties. As they talked, however, she was confident that Anthony was in good hands because Kelsey Seybold hired only the best. He took her into his office, his face grim. Nadia feared the worst.

"What is actually wrong, doctor?" Nadia's hands were tightly wound in her lap, her nerves a wreck. She tried to fight back tears. "Is it that bad?"

"I am talking to you only because Anthony requested that I discuss everything about his illness with you, just so you know. His ex-wife has been here, but I guessed from her behavior that she didn't really care for him, despite her concern."

"We're supposed to be getting married," Nadia said, knowing at that very moment that she didn't really want to waste another minute she could be spending with someone she loved. Nick's death had been sudden, painful, and despite the love they shared, she wished there were possibly more ways she could have shown her love. Whatever Anthony had going on, she would be there for him when it was all over.

"Really? God." He was quiet for a minute. "There's no easy way to do this, but Anthony has kidney disease, end stage renal disease, to be specific."

"What? How? He is a healthy guy!"

"I know, but these things just happen like this sometimes, and there's no explanation for them. But thank God, he checked himself into the hospital as soon as he knew something was terribly wrong. Smart man."

Nadia was puzzled. "Isn't he supposed to have symptoms? I mean…how could he just develop kidney disease like that?"

"There are lots of symptoms, but sometimes the busyness of life makes us not pay close attention to our bodies. Swelling of the feet, ankles, and hands, change in urination patterns, fatigue or weakness, back pain, among others. He might have been feeling these with other things and not particularly paying attention. He's a very busy man, so it's understandable. He has had high blood pressure for years, but that has been well managed. Still, these things happen without warning sometimes."

"Is he going to be OK?"

"We are running tests at the moment. He should be up and awake though anytime now. We'd have to keep him here to make sure everything is all right, before we decide on the course of treatment."

"So, it's treatable?"

"Depends on the stage. I'm hoping all we'd have to do is hemodialysis."

"Wow…that word alone…doesn't sound good at all, Dr. Livingston." Unbidden tears streamed down her cheeks. "Oh my God, Anthony."

"Now, now, Ms. Gardner, let's be optimistic, OK? I can assure you that the worst is over." Just then, he was alerted that Anthony was awake. "Let's go," he said to Nadia.

Indeed, Anthony was up and cheerful, a far cry from what Nadia had seen earlier. Kate was talking to him.

"Nadia!" He extended his hands. Some of the gadgets had been disconnected. "You're here."

"Yes." She took his hand and sat beside him on the bed. "David called me last night. I was beginning to worry!"

"How are you feeling?" Dr. Livingston asked.

"Better. A little bit sore all over."

"That will pass. Let me go check on your results. The sooner we know what we're up against, the better."

Anthony turned to Nadia. "You're not leaving yet?"

"I'll stay here all day if I have to."

The doctor smiled. "OK. I'll be back."

"Why didn't you call me earlier? Emmett's been going out of his mind, too."

"I couldn't. Tell him Dad will be well soon."

"Dad? What do you mean, Dad? Who is Emmett?" Kate yelled, unconcerned that they were in a hospital room.

"Now is not the time please," Nadia implored. "Please, let's just concentrate on making sure that Anthony gets better."

"Anthony, who is Emmett?" she looked at Nadia with unabashed scorn.

"This is really not the time for this, but since you're so insistent, Emmett is my son. Nadia's and my son. He is fifteen."

"What?"

"And that's all I'm going to say for now," Anthony ground out. "Please can you give us some space?"

"You're just going to ask me to leave just because she's here?"

"I'm just asking for you to give us some privacy, OK?"

Kate glared at Nadia as she angrily walked out of the room. "Whatever."

"Wow…all that hatred cannot be good for her blood pressure. Why hasn't she ever tried to get along?"

"She'll come around some day," Anthony said. He looked weak, but his grip on her arm was firm. "Give me a kiss."

She obliged, brushing his lips lightly with hers. "I was really worried. Where are the girls?"

"Staying with their mother for the time being."

"Has she brought them by?"

"No, I told her not to for now. Besides, I might be going home soon. I don't want the kids to see me like this. I hope you didn't think I absconded again, Nadia." He searched her face for a glimpse of her feelings.

"It's not easy. I did at first, but then decided not to jump to conclusions. If David hadn't called, I probably would have called him this morning."

"I would never do that to you again, Nadia. This time I'm here to stay."

"All is well. You looked so helpless when I came in earlier. How come you didn't catch the symptoms earlier? Kidney disease is not something to joke with."

"Too busy chasing things, I guess. I wouldn't have forgiven myself if anything happened to me."

"Nothing will happen to you. Dr. Livingston should soon be back with your test results. You need to get well so we can get married like you want to and raise those children together."

The doctor came in then with a file folder in his hand. "It's not looking good" was all he said.

"We can afford any kind of treatment, doctor," Nadia said.

"It's not a matter of money, Ms. Gardner. Mr. Okafor definitely needs a new kidney."

CHAPTER EIGHT

Oh God!" Kate, who just walked back into the room, gasped.

Anthony handled it pretty well under the circumstances. His face was devoid of any emotion, but his eyes were red. "I need a transplant?"

"There's no other choice," Dr. Livingston answered. "And it has to be done within the next three months. You have ESRD or End Stage Renal Disease, Mr. Okafor, so we need to make haste about a treatment plan."

Nadia didn't know how she stayed calm. She wanted to do many things: throw herself at Anthony and cry, bang her head against the wall, ask God why life was so unfair, but was a picture of calm and resilience.

"What is the next possible thing to do?" she asked the doctor.

"Of course, we'll start hemodialysis immediately, but we'll also have to start looking for possible donors. I'll put his name in the registry but also test family members to see if we'll find a match."

"Oh my God, Anthony!" Kate rushed to his bedside. "I'm sorry...so sorry." She sobbed uncontrollably. "You're too young for this...why now?"

"It's OK, sis. I'll be fine."

"I have to call Mom and Dad and tell them."

"No!" he said. "Don't do any such thing. All you'll do is get them worried. I want to keep this as private as possible."

"I don't know how possible that will be considering that we have to ask willing donors to be tested," Dr. Livingston stated.

"I want to be tested right away," Nadia volunteered. "Kate, how about you?"

The other lady nodded, still at a loss for words. She looked helpless for once, and Nadia was tempted to give her hug but decided against it.

"Can I see you in my office for a moment?" Dr. Livingston said to Nadia. "Anthony, I'll be back to check on you momentarily."

Anthony looked at Nadia. "OK."

"It's not looking really good, Ms. Gardner, but there's still a lot of time to correct things, so I won't mince words," the doctor said to Nadia in his office. "We have to act fast to find a match. So, I'm going to task you with rallying those who you think might want to donate a kidney. It's not an easy decision by any means. Do you know anything about the disease?"

She shook her head. "Only a little bit. You never think something like this would happen to your loved one."

"Certainly. Well, obviously it negatively affects the body because the kidney is unable to effectively remove excess waste and water, its primary functions. High blood pressure is a contributing factor, and Mr. Okafor has had that for three years."

"I didn't even know he had high blood pressure."

"That's an easily manageable illness, so there's no alarm. I have to have a list of possible donors in two days' time, I will give you a number, and they can also call the hospital directly to book an appointment to come get themselves tested." His voice softened as he watched Nadia's face and the emotions she was battling. "He'll be all right, Ms. Gardner. Mr. Okafor is a strong man. We can only pray and act fast and hope to get a match soon."

Emmett was devastated by the news but calmed down after lots of assurances from his parents. It hurt Nadia to see him so pained so soon after reconciling with his dad, and she talked to him a lot so he wouldn't lose focus in school and sports activities. Anthony's girls were staying with Sara in the meantime, and Anthony was provided a full-time nurse to help him with hemodialysis and daily activities. It wasn't hard to find volunteers to be tested, but there was still no match after a week. Anthony was optimistic, however, and Nadia admired his resolve and determination to beat the disease.

He took time off from the firm to focus on himself, and even Kenneth paid him a couple of visits. It all seemed like a bad dream to Nadia. It wasn't conceivable to her how this could happen to the Anthony she now realized she loved. She didn't know if she could handle losing Anthony, especially after the way Nick died. As much faith as she had in God, she knew her faith was being tested. How could God allow this to happen?

Anthony's illness really made her reflect on her life's journey. It seemed that she never caught a break without another obstacle rising in her path. Her childhood was marred by her father's authoritarian rule of his household, and her teenage years by restrictive religious rules that made it impossible to have fun like her peers. Anthony had betrayed her love for him by disappearing after a weekend of passion that left her pregnant, and just as she was thinking that life couldn't possibly better, Nick had passed in that terrible car accident. Even though her outlook on religion and spiritually was a far cry from what it used to be, she believed she had a personal relationship to God and tried to fathom a way to draw closer to Him rather than questioning the events in her life. After all, other people went through the same things, some even worse.

Nadia checked in with Dr. Livingston often to get updates on the treatment and possible matches. She avoided thinking about the situation too much yet prayed daily to God for a miracle. Everybody she knew had been tested: Kate, David, Scott Brenner, Kenneth, Kenneth's parents, Angela, and even Lizzy. The direness of the situation alone drove her to tears every night before bed.

"Don't look so worried," said Anthony, who was lying in a recliner watching TV. She was on the couch going through some paperwork while spending time with him before she went home.

"I'm not worried."

"I can see through you, Nadia. Don't be so tough on yourself. Do your best and leave the rest to God."

"Oh Anthony, why us? I mean, why now? Not many people get second chances at love like we did."

"We are getting a second chance." He came to sit beside her. "Every moment we spend together should be cherished." He nuzzled his face in her hair. "I love you, Nadia."

"It's just so unfair," she sobbed into his chest.

"I will get better, Nadia," he proclaimed. "Together we can beat this." He held her face in his hands. "We will spend the rest of our lives together with these kids, and any others we might have."

"We haven't had any matches. It's been four weeks, Anthony. Even Dr. Livingston is starting to sound desperate."

"I don't think so. He is one of the most rock-solid people I know."

"We need a miracle, love."

"God is a God of miracles. I know all will be OK. Now stop worrying, OK?"

"I love you so much!"

"I love you, too. Emmett called me earlier. I'm wishing we hadn't told him about this," he regretted. "He was asking for us to give him permission to go get tested."

Nadia tensed immediately. "What?"

"I thought I hadn't heard right at first. I told him he's doing no such thing. I just can't imagine being in his shoes at this moment. I couldn't have prayed for a better son."

Nadia was quiet. It never occurred to her to think of Emmett as a possible donor. The thought alone sent shockwaves through her body. There was no way she was letting him consider being a donor. She got up abruptly, needing to get away from Anthony and clear her head.

"I've got to go make dinner, Anthony. I'll see you tomorrow, OK?" She kissed him lightly on the lips. "You want me to call the nurse for you?"

"I'm good."

"I bet you can't complain," she said, "You have two beautiful women spoiling you at the moment."

"Are you kidding me? I can say that about the nurse but not about Roberta. She's almost sixty years old!"

Nadia laughed. "Just checking. Anyways, don't let her hear you say that."

The Spanish nanny treated Nadia like a daughter and was always begging her to eat her home made chili con queso. Despite the girls not being there, she prepared most of Anthony's meals under the nurse's direction. Dr. Livingston had put Anthony on a special diet that included lots of vegetables, fruits, low sodium, increased protein, and complete avoidance of calcium and phosphorus.

"I'll see you tomorrow, love."

Nadia let herself out the door. The ride home was anything but pleasant. She couldn't believe Emmett would approach Anthony with such a proposition without telling her first. She marched straight upstairs to his room upon getting home.

"Why didn't you tell me you were going to ask to be tested?" she demanded. "How could you do that to me Emmett?"

"Mom, I just wanted to help."

"You should have run it by me first. Besides I am not going to let you do that."

"What if I come out as a match?"

"You are too young, Emmett. You have your whole life ahead of you and you can't be donating your kidney to nobody."

"Mom, this is for my dad, in case you have forgotten. I thought you loved him."

"Now, you look here, this has nothing to do with love. You are too young. Period." Nadia was exasperated. "Why are you doing this to me, Emmett? Why? This is how you pay me back after all these years?"

"Mom, he is my dad!" Emmett almost screamed at her, shocking both of them into somberness. That was the first time he had ever raised his voice to her. "I haven't had a dad for fifteen years, and now that I have one, he is going to die," he said brokenly.

"He is not going to die, baby. Come here." Nadia hugged him tight. "Everything will be all right, you'll see. I understand how you feel, but I can't stand the risk of losing the two men I love. Let's pray that your father will find a match soon." She released him slowly but held on to his arms. "I love you, OK? You should have told me, though,"

He nodded, too emotional to speak. "I love you, Mom."

"I'll go make dinner. You want anything in particular?"

"Mashed potatoes."

"OK, mashed potatoes it is. Now go freshen up and get your stuff ready for tomorrow."

"Right, Mom. I'm sorry I didn't talk to you first, before I told Dad. It just came out while we were on the phone."

"It's all right. Forget about it."

Nadia didn't get a good sleep that night, though. With Emmett's insistence on helping his dad the enormity of the situation finally hit her. Certainly, she wouldn't have hesitated to do the same except she wasn't compatible with what Dr. Livingston was looking for. As usual, she cried herself to sleep, unable to hold back her feelings in the private comfort of her room.

She was in the office three days later when a call came in from Dr. Livingston.

"Nadia." He had stopped calling her Ms. Gardner a long time ago. There was just too much at stake to be bothered with formalities, and he had become a kind of confidant for her unbridled emotions sometimes. "We got a match."

"Oh my God, that is good news!" she exclaimed, springing up from her chair. "Oh my God, I can't believe this."

"Yes, I was beginning to worry myself. The list is swamped, and it's a first-come-first-serve basis. Anthony is a very lucky man."

"Who is it?"

"Emmett."

Nadia's heart sank, and Dr. Livingston could feel the turmoil in her.

"Nadia, he is in fact the most perfect match. But we can't do anything without your consent. And Anthony has to agree to want it, too."

"Wow!" Nadia couldn't comprehend anything at all.

"Nadia?"

"But the risks are too great," she voiced at last. "Emmett is too young."

"Really, he is not. It's a very tough decision." Dr. Livingston would not cajole nor discourage. "I'll talk to you later, OK?"

"Yes. Thanks, doctor."

"You bet."

Nadia could only think of one person to call under the circumstances. "Liz."

"Hey, girl, what's wrong?" Lizzy sensed her distress right away. "Is it Anthony?"

"Yes and no. Do you know that Emmett went behind my back to get tested, and the doctor just called me because he is a match?"

"Wow!" The news flabbergasted Lizzy, too. "Does Anthony know?"

"I haven't told him. Lizzy, what am I going to do? This is just crazy."

"Calm down, Nadia. This is a two-edged sword however you look at it. If you don't let Emmett do it and anything happens to Anthony, he will never forgive you. If he goes ahead and does it, God forbid that any complications arise, you will blame yourself and it might even damage the relationship between you and Anthony forever. Either way you have to give it careful thought."

"The doctor said Anthony could refuse."

"Ah…it's a touchy situation indeed. For once, I'm at a loss for words. How is the situation with Kate?" Everybody knew Anthony's sister's feelings where Nadia was concerned.

"That one? I just ignore her. I have a feeling she's secretly blaming Anthony's illness on me."

"That's foolish."

"Can you argue with a fool? Anyway I just avoid her whenever we cross paths at Anthony's place. And her husband is a very nice quiet man, God knows how he puts up with her."

"Love is blind."

"Indeed," Nadia concurred. "Thanks so much, Liz. I actually feel lighter after talking to you. I'll have to call on God for this one."

"For everything in fact. See you later. I'll try come by this weekend. I've really missed our lunches."

"Me too. Thanks for your understanding. Bye."

When Nadia's phone rang at two thirty am, she knew it wouldn't be good news. An early morning call was usually from Nigeria, and her family knew the time difference enough to know they could not call so early unless it was an emergency.

Groggily, she picked up the call. It was her younger brother Jaleel. Their father was ill, and she needed to come home immediately.

"Is it that serious?"

"Yes,"

"I'll call you later in the day." She hung up feeling deflated and tired. She hadn't been back home in fifteen years, but how could she possibly leave Anthony to go to Nigeria at this time when he needed her most?

She needn't have worried however. She felt confident handing the reins of KNG Corporation to Kenneth and Debbie, who were two very capable hands, in the meantime but then there was Emmett. This was a good opportunity for him to visit Nigeria, but he wanted to stay with his dad. She didn't think it was a good idea, though Anthony welcomed the news with enthusiasm, knowing it would be a good opportunity to strengthen the bond between father and son. He completely understood her predicament and urged her to travel to Nigeria to see her father and the other family members she hadn't seen in such a long time. She got ready for the trip with firm assurance from Dr. Livingston that Anthony was in good shape for now and was on a United Airlines direct flight to Lagos within the week.

Her flight companion was a white businessman in his mid-fifties. He cracked her up with his knowledge of Lagos and other Nigerian states he had visited and spoke the Igbo language like a native. He had stakes in oil and gas in Delta State, including a successful cement factory in Ogun State. His family lived in Nigeria, but he travelled often and was in the process of setting up a private school in Lagos.

He also had heard of KNG Corporation. When Nadia told him about the scholarships, he suggested a possible future educational collaboration between them. Nadia couldn't have been more thrilled. They exchanged business cards. Lagos was soon below them, and Nadia was hit by nostalgia. It was hard to believe that so much had changed in fifteen years.

The first thing that hit her when she got off the plane was the humidity. The second was the cacophony of noise as she made her way through customs and retrieved her luggage, which took an endless three hours. Different men kept approaching her asking to offer assistance, but she declined. When she finally stepped out into the hot Nigerian sun, she was glad she had followed Anthony's advice and worn a T-shirt and jeans with sneakers. When a young man approached her, she almost flinched, until he called her name.

"Sister Nadia." It was her brother Jaleel, the third born of her mother. "Sister Nadia, it's me, Jaleel."

"Jaleel!" she exclaimed as she hugged him. "Oh my God, you're all grown up!"

"Yes." He laughed excitedly and helped her get her luggage in the trunk. "Let's get in the car. This place is crowded, and I don't want to keep paying these area boys to keep my space."

Lagos certainly looked different than she remembered. Everybody was on a cell phone. Everybody was in trendy fashion, and most were in jeans and T-shirts like one would see in Houston on a hot summer day. If not for the poor environmental maintenance on the roads, disorganized infrastructure, and pictures of poverty she saw by the roadside as they drove home, she would have thought she was in any suburban city in the United States. Her conclusion was that while the people of Nigeria had progressed exponentially as a people, Nigeria herself had digressed exponentially as a nation. This couldn't be further from the truth as they drove along potholes as big as the state of Texas, angry drivers that didn't have qualms about driving against traffic, and she was shocked when even the mild Jaleel she knew cursed at a driver for cutting him off in traffic.

As they approached Festac Town, she was at a loss for words on how degenerate the once beautiful town looked. Houses and makeshift shacks were crammed into every nook and corner. Even the beautiful parks she used to play in as a kid were nonexistent amidst the juxtaposition of unplanned buildings that made no sense whatsoever. It was as if the devil was given a carte blanche to "undesign" the town and had done a very good job at it. Nobody she recognized was outside. All the houses had gates, and some of the gates were almost seven feet tall. Jaleel explained that the gates were necessary to keep out robbers.

"Is it that bad?"

"Better safe than sorry, sis. That's the situation of Festac Town at the moment."

Her mother and other family members flooded out to greet her as Jaleel took care of her luggage. "Nadia, where is your scarf?"

"Scarf? Mom, you don't expect me to tie a scarf around my head, do you?"

"Please, just for your father. You can do whatever you want when you leave the house."

"Mom—"

"Please," her mother implored. "You know he's not feeling good. Don't add to his sickness. Let one of the girls go get you a scarf, OK?"

Nadia shook her head. Just like old times. She was seriously thinking about checking into a hotel. There were too many people in the house already anyway. She had envisaged her dad frail and helpless on a bed, but he looked surprisingly spritely in a chair in the living room. She embraced him lightly and sat down. He didn't look a day older than he was before she travelled.

Why all the urgency? she asked herself. She soon found out. It had just been a prostate cancer scare, nothing more. And the symptoms had been cleared up with herbal medicine. Nadia was glad to be back home but refused to stay at the house. She settled on a midsize hotel just outside of Festac Town. It was expensive, but the room was clean and the jollof rice was out of this world.

As soon as she was unpacked, she called Anthony and Emmett, who were glad she landed safely. They missed her already and couldn't wait for her to come back home.

The next few days saw a flurry of visitors in and out of her room, including Grace, her best friend from childhood. She brought gifts for everyone and gave substantial money to Grace to open a fast-food restaurant in Festac Town. She got in touch with Dr. Livingston. Anthony was holding up well, but they only had so much time before a transplant could take place. All her motherly instincts went against Emmett's decision, but then Anthony was Emmett's father and the love of her life. She was really between a rock and a hard place, and it wasn't made easier by a visit from none other than Aunt Edna.

It was well into her second week, and she was alone in her room just after breakfast when the knock came on the door. They were both shocked to see each other. Nadia started closing the door.

"Nadia, we need to talk," the older woman said.

"About what?"

"Can I come in?"

"Whatever you want to say can be said here," Nadia said. "I'm very busy."

"It's about Anthony."

Nadia's heart sank just briefly. He was in good spirits when they spoke earlier. She opened the door wider to let her in. "Come in."

Aunt Edna sat perched on the edge of the sofa. "Nadia, let me start by begging your forgiveness. With age comes wisdom, and I know the cruel words I said to you twenty years ago must have hurt."

"There's nothing to forgive, Aunt Edna. To dwell on the past is a waste of precious time."

"True. But the past must sometimes be revisited to make right the present and future. I shouldn't have said those things to you regardless. It actually wasn't my place."

"It's OK. I'm good." Nadia was sitting on the bed. "How's your family doing?"

"Good. I came to talk to you about something very important."

"Anthony."

"Kate told me about his illness. And Anthony told me about the son you both have together. You know I have always been close to him. He is my favorite nephew."

"He can take care of himself, too," Nadia opined.

"He also said that Emmett offered to be tested."

"So? I can't even believe you people are suggesting what I'm thinking. You all want me to sacrifice my son for Anthony? Have you forgotten what you told me years ago? That Anthony is not my type, and I should stick with my type? And then I get to the US and he ships me off to a roommate after promising he'll help me get on my feet. It's not that pleasant when the tables are turned, isn't it?"

Aunt Edna's shoulders dropped. "Nadia, please forgive and forget."

"I did that a long time ago. You have children too, Aunt Edna. How would you feel, knowing   the risks involved, to allow any child of yours to do that? I don't know. I just don't know."

"I understand." Aunt Edna stood up. "I have to go. I'm glad we talked. Think about it, OK?"

Nadia didn't answer. Her bravado was convincing, but she was distraught on the inside. She felt Anthony's parents might have put Aunt Edna up to it, though she wasn't sure. How ironic life could be.

"How was your trip?" Kenneth asked. He was the only one available to pick her from George Bush International Airport in the early hours of the morning on her arrival back to the United States. "Is your dad feeling better?"

Nadia smiled. "It was OK. So many things have changed. Wow! All my siblings are so grown and having babies. My nieces and nephews kept calling me 'Big Mommy' and insisted on following me everywhere. I even had to let them sleep in my hotel room for a couple of days. The girls especially. I can tell you I only came back with what I'm wearing and two pairs of shoes. They 'borrowed' everything except my underwear. It was fun, though. And my dad, false alarm. He's as agile as I've ever seen him. It sure was good to see old faces again."

"I went to see Anthony yesterday."

"Thanks, Kenneth. You really have done a lot and more. How is he?"

"Good. He keeps a brave face especially for Emmett, but I could see his pain. I'm so sorry, Nadia, to have this happen to you. Life," he sighed.

"You know Emmett's a match," she revealed. "The doctor called me just before I travelled. He had gone and gotten tested without telling me."

"What are you going to do?"

"It's a hard decision. I don't want to lose my son, but I don't have a choice but to give consent since he wants to do it."

"All will be well, Nadia. I'm sure." Kenneth patted her on the shoulder. "You want to make any stops before I drop you at Anthony's place?"

"What gave you the idea I would want to go to Anthony's place?" she said jokingly, smiling. "You guys are just taking over like it's your right. Well, I'm going there, but you can drop me at home. I need to pick up some clothes and get my car."

She also needed some time to ponder her decision to finally grant Emmett's wishes. If she didn't consent and they lost Anthony to ESRD, then it was as good as losing both of them because things would never be the same between her and Emmett again and that was a notion she couldn't even begin to consider.

She knew they would be expecting her since the first thing she did was call them as soon as she landed at the airport. Emmett had groggily answered the phone, but Anthony was already up early, watching the news. She could tell that he missed her terribly as he almost didn't want to hang up until she promised to get there as soon as she could. The house was just as she left it, except for one of Emmett's jackets on the living room couch. The first thing she did was unpack some of the spices she brought from Africa for proper storage, then took a good one-hour shower to hydrate her tired body. There were six missed calls from Anthony when she got out of the shower.

"Everything OK?" she asked when she returned his call.

"Where are you?"

"At home. Taking a much-needed shower and packing some clothes. I'll be there within the hour."

"All right. Hurry up, woman. I've missed you so much…" His voice trailed away. "I don't want to lose any more precious time, Nadia."

"Please, Anthony, it hasn't come to that. I'll be there within the hour."

"All right."

Life was funny, Nadia thought on hanging up. Would Anthony have behaved differently if he knew the future? Would she have met and experienced the wonderful love she had with Nick when Anthony abandoned her? How would the scenario have played out if she had gotten rid of Emmett? What if she was the perfect match needed for the transplant and his one hope of survival? What if they had never bumped into each other at the mall or become business colleagues? She went on and on and on in a whirlwind of thoughts, so much so that she was already pulling into Anthony's driveway before she realized it. Emmett came bounding out of the house even before she was parked.

"Mom, you're back!" He almost knocked her down in his enthusiasm.

"Easy now." She steadied herself as she hugged him back. "Can you get my duffel? It's in the trunk." She followed him. "How have you guys coped without me?"

"I think we did pretty well, with the nurse and Roberta's help of course. I'm beginning to watch my weight 'cos she's always feeding me, Mom. The girls have been coming around, too."

"Hmm…I thought your dad didn't want them to know."

"He couldn't stand not seeing them. And they didn't break down like he thought they would. Strong girls, Erin and Yazmine."

Emmett retrieved her bag and looked her straight in the eye. "I'm going to do it, Mom."

"I know you are," she replied quietly. "You're very brave, Emmett."

He stood for a second trying to comprehend her words. Then his face lit up in a big smile. "I can?"

Nadia nodded. "Yes."

"Oh, you're the best mom ever!" Emmett shouted in glee, dropping the bag to hug her tightly. "I know you're worried, but we'll come out fine OK, Mom?"

"I know. Come on, let's go tell your dad the good news."

Anthony's reaction was not what they were expecting at all. He was furious at Emmett for getting tested without his mom's knowledge, and then he adamantly refused to let him donate a kidney. "No, son, I'm not letting you do that. You are too young, and it's too risky."

"I've already discussed it with Dr. Livingston," Nadia assured. "You're the only one we need to get on board now, and we're good to go."

"Can we discuss this upstairs?" Anthony said to Nadia.

"I've made my decision, Anthony," Nadia told him out of earshot. "It's a difficult situation, and it will be either win-win or lose-lose. I am not ready to lose either of you right now."

"I'm concerned for Emmett," Anthony stated matter-of-factly. "He just barely began to live life. And you must be crazy to give in to this, too. I want to be well and healthy but not at the expense of my only son."

"And how do you expect me to feel?" Nadia whispered. "This is so hard."

"Come here." He pulled her into his arms. "God…you smell so fresh. I can't even imagine my life without you, Nadia. However, things turn out. I was a fool for letting you go fifteen years ago."

Her arms went around his waist as she nuzzled against his chest. "It's OK. I have to call Dr. Livingston first thing in the morning."

He pulled back, looking deep into her eyes. "You sure? I am really sorry, Nadia, for all you went through. I wish things had been different. And you have raised a remarkable young man, really. I couldn't have asked for a better son."

"It's all right. It took a while but I've never been surer of anything in my life. Sometimes you just have to take the bull by the horns and hope for the best." She smiled at him.

"Spoken like a true CEO," he quipped.

"More like a mother and a lover."

"We're not lovers yet, though we can start changing that status right now." He kissed her soundly on the lips.

"Oh no, nothing until all this is cleared up, and I am Mrs. Okafor."

"You don't have to change your name, you know. I wish I'd met Nick. He sounds like a remarkable person."

"He was," Nadia said simply. "He will always have a special place in my heart."

"I'm not even going to attempt to take his place, Nadia, so long as I have my own special place, too."

"Yes." She placed his hand on her chest.

He could feel the rhythmic beat of her heart against his hand. Slowly, he placed his lips on hers.

CHAPTER NINE

Nadia was deep in thought as she looked out the hospital window. She was scared to turn and face the other family members in the private waiting room. Almost everybody had come to show their support for Anthony and Emmett while they underwent the three-to four-hour transplant operation. Kenneth and Vera, Keira, David, Lizzy, Lorraine, Rakhya, Angela, and Kate.

It had taken two weeks before all the preparations and secondary tests were finalized to make sure both father and son could withstand the rigorousness of the procedure. In addition, Dr. Livingston had to make sure that there was minimal chance a rejection would occur, although this really was an uncontrollable side effect.

Nadia checked her watch. It was almost three and a half hours in, and nobody had come to tell them anything yet. She began to worry. She sighed heavily as she fought tears from streaming down her cheeks. The two most important people in her life were both under the mercy of God and doctor's knives, and there was nothing she could do about it. She felt a gentle hand on her shoulder. It was Rakhya. She covered the hand with her own, willingly basking in offered comfort.

"They'll be all right, sis. I promise you," Rakhya soothed.

"It's almost four hours, Rakhya."

"I know, but I know Dr. Livingston knows what he's doing. And God is in control."

"Then why did this happen?" Nadia whispered. "If God is in control, why did this have to happen to Anthony?"

"Sis! Please don't talk like that. You know better, sis, or you wouldn't have taken both of them to church and asked the pastor to pray for them before the surgery. Sometimes, we cannot choose the burdens that come to us, but we must carry them nonetheless, and pray that they are not too much to bear. And God did promise that no burden He gives us will be too much to bear."

"I'm just tired Rakhya, I don't want to lose either of them."

"You won't. Come and sit down." Rakhya led her to a chair amidst sympathetic looks from the others.

"Is she OK?" asked Kate.

"She's fine," Rakhya replied shortly, Nadia knew how Rakhya felt about Anthony's sister and hoped she would keep things in check considering the situation.

Kate's mouth tightened but she refrained from saying anything. Just then, Dr. Livingston walked into the room, smiling.

He stood looking at all of them for a minute, then settled his gaze on Nadia. "The operation was a success. Both men are fine and doing well. However, they cannot accept visitors now except close family members and just for a few minutes."

"Thank God!"

Everybody hugged each other amidst congratulating the doctor, who was beaming from ear to ear as if he just had a baby. Nadia couldn't wait one more second. It was with relief that she and Kate followed Dr. Livingston out of the room. Anthony and Emmett were still in the same room in separate beds. Love welled up in Nadia's heart. She ran between the beds and held each of their hands, while Kate went by Emmett's bed and gave him a kiss on the forehead, which surprised Nadia.

"Thank you, son," she said.

"It's God," Emmett said, looking up at his mother. Nadia felt like hugging both of them right there. The tears she had tried so hard to hold back came spilling down, so hard that Dr. Livingston had to comfort her and lead her out of the room.

"It's all right, Nadia. You can see they're both fine," he assured her as he led her back to the waiting room. "They have to be here several days, so we can monitor them and make sure everything is OK. Then they will be ready to come home."

"I'm just so happy. Thank you, Dr. Livingston. Thank you so much."

Only Kenneth and Vera were left in the waiting room. Nadia thanked them and implored them to leave to get some rest, especially as she could see that Vera was getting tired. She was already in her thirtieth week and looked ready to have the baby any moment.

"You have a very loving family, Nadia." Dr. Livingston said.

"Yes, I'm indeed lucky. When will they be ready to receive regular visitors?"

"About two days. We want to make sure they get plenty of rest, and Emmett should start walking around and doing some light exercise by then. We are more concerned for Anthony in case of a possible rejection, but for now everything looks good."

"I really appreciate your support, doctor."

"You're welcome, Nadia." He patted her on the shoulder. "I've got to go get ready for another surgery. Feel free to call me anytime, OK? And I'll call you if anything crops up, which is unlikely."

She smiled and hugged. "Thank you."

"No problem," Dr. Livingston said and left.

Nadia sank in one of the plush chairs, relaxed for the first time in months.

"Nadia, I need to talk to you," said Kate, who looked happier than before the surgery.

Nadia still didn't trust her, though. She tensed. "What about?"

"I want to thank you for letting Emmett do this. He is a very brave young man. We will forever be grateful to him."

"Anthony is his dad. All is well."

"There's something else I want to discuss with you, though, I—" Kate was interrupted by her phone ringing. She talked to the caller for a few minutes. "I'm so sorry Nadia, I have to go. Work. But I'll definitely call you because what I want to say is important."

"OK." Nadia's reply was nonchalant because she couldn't fathom what it was about. "Drive safely."

"Thanks. You too take care. I hope you're going to go home and get some sleep."

"I am. I'm just going to relax here for a while and then be on my way."

"All right. See you later."

Nadia went to work the next day late after a good rest. She had gone to her house to be alone, and it did her a lot of good. She cried some more, laughed, prayed, and constantly thanked God for answering her prayers. She had a long bath, called Lizzy, made a light dinner, and fell asleep while watching TV on the living room couch. She went to work the next day feeling on top of the world.

An important meeting engaged her for about two hours until ten. She stopped by all the departments to mingle with staff, then retired to her office for a break. By the time she got back, her pile of daily mail and newspapers were already stacked neatly on a tray. As she sat down something caught her eye. It was a headline in the *Houston Herald*. "High School Sophomore Donates Kidney to Save Father." Nadia couldn't believe her eyes. Everybody had been sworn to secrecy about Anthony's illness especially as Brenner and

Okafor did not want their clients getting worried because he was ill. She called Kenneth.

"Can you come to my office?"

"What's wrong Nadia?" Kenneth was anxious. "Wow," he said when he saw the story. "How could it have gone out? Somebody snitched."

"I have no idea who it could be. You think it's Kate?"

He shook his head. "Nope. She couldn't do such a thing. Wait, it may be Sara."

"Sara, Anthony's ex-wife? What does she stand to gain from this?"

"Money talks, Nadia. Don't let it upset you, though. I'll make some inquiries and get back to you. Do you mind if I hold on to this?"

"Not at all, just make sure I get it back. Anthony would be furious."

"It's not really a negative story," Kenneth pointed out. "I'm thinking greed is behind this. Not to worry. I'll get to the bottom of it." He left with the newspaper.

It galled Nadia that Sara would disclose the information to the *Herald* for money. She visited Anthony only twice in the hospital and wasn't even present on the day of the surgery, giving an excuse that she had a prescheduled visit out of town. She came across as a nice lady, but sometimes Nadia could see shallowness and selfishness in her actions and behavior. She knew that even if they hadn't divorced because of her cheating ways, Anthony would have gotten rid of her sooner or later. He might have his faults, but shallowness and selfishness were not among them.

Nadia called Scott Brenner. He had seen the article too and already done a quick preliminary investigation through another law firm. "I think she might be doing this, so she can have custody of the girls."

"But she didn't want the girls," Nadia said. "How could she be doing this? She could have discussed it with Anthony instead of broadcasting the state of his health to the world."

"You never know with some women, Nadia. I'm very sure that is the motive, so she can prove that Anthony might not be capable of taking care of the girls himself."

"That's what nannies are for, and even before he fell sick, they had a nanny."

"Some people don't think things through, Nadia. Any argument she starts won't hold up in court. Thousands of people go on living normal lives after a transplant."

"Anyway, I called to make you aware of the story."

"We're good over here. Emmett comes out as quite the hero. Good boy you both have there, Nadia. I hope they both get well soon."

"Yes, thanks, Scott."

"You bet. Bye now,"

Further investigation indeed showed that Sara had leaked the story to the paper.

Anthony wasn't surprised by Sara's betrayal. "You know we settled our divorce through arbitration. She's been asking for more money just because she's currently taking care of the girls while I'm in the hospital, and I've obliged her. I guess she figures why give the girls back when she could keep them. She's even threatening to go to court. I just don't get it."

"Why don't you just let her have the girls then?" Nadia probed. "She'll have to keep them for a while so you can get better."

"What about you Nadia? Why can't you keep the girls?"

"Anthony, you know I wouldn't hesitate, but right now we need to concentrate on getting you and Emmett on a healthy path. I wouldn't be able to divide my time between both of you and the girls. And how am I going to do that without hiring a nanny?"

"You could move in with me."

"Oh no, we are not married yet. And what kind of example are we setting for the kids by doing that anyway? Let Sara keep the girls and tell her to give you time to get better."

"Haven't you noticed how she behaves? I don't want Erin and Yazmine to pick up her bad habits. And now that she's even more money-hungry." He shook his head in disappointment. "I don't want to end up with a pair of brats who think they can have whatever they want."

"Erin and Yazmine are more sensible than that from what I've seen. You shouldn't be so worried, though, they are still in Houston, not Timbuktu."

Nadia had developed a fondness for the girls since they were introduced on one of their visits to Anthony. They were cool as teenagers could be toward her initially but had gradually mellowed on realizing their dad was committed to Nadia.

"True, but you can't blame me for being worried. Have you seen Emmett?" Emmett had been moved to another section of the hospital for recovery.

"Yes, he's doing really well. He can't wait to go back to school and sports, though it's going to be awhile before he can play. Is this room not too cold for you?" She shivered as cool air hit her body.

"I like it this way. Even the nurse was asking me if it was too cold. To me, it's just right. You can get a blanket from the cabinet if you're that cold."

"It's OK." Nadia was sitting on the edge of his bed, and she placed a kiss on his lips. "Can't wait for you to come home. Dr. Livingston says you'll be good to go in a couple more days. Emmett is leaving tomorrow."

"To your place or mine."

"Yours, of course. Wouldn't make sense to have him stay with me when there's a nurse and nanny that he's comfortable with already at your house. He doesn't really need the nurse, but I'll take Roberta with me if you don't mind."

Anthony laughed. "Oh no, not Roberta. She's a lifesaver for when the girls come around. Don't know what I would do without her. That's settled then, and once I get better, we'll get married."

"You know, the day of the surgery Kate said she had something to tell me, but she was called back to work before she could say it. Do you have any idea what it might be?"

Anthony tensed just for a second then shrugged. "Why don't you call her?"

"Don't want to be too inquisitive. She said she would call me but she hasn't, and I don't want to press the issue. It's all right. Whenever she's ready."

Nadia stayed another hour before taking her leave, albeit reluctantly. She and Anthony had never really spent much time together until lately, and she really enjoyed his company.

There had been several florist deliveries to her office that he orchestrated even from his hospital bed, and he seemed to take her feelings into consideration now before he acted. He even apologized to her for repeatedly barging into her office when she told him not to when they first reconnected. He was a very intelligent man who seemed to have a solution to any problem.

Several times she wanted to ask him for the real reason behind his disappearing act at the time Emmett was conceived, but she didn't want to start another war especially in his condition. That was one hurdle she had to clear before she married him. He professed his love without any inhibitions which only created a well of questions in her head as to what really happened, and she was starting to think his family might have been behind it.

She was back at work by four to put in a couple of hours and catch up with her paperwork. Kenneth was still in the office.

"Nadia." He smiled. "I guess the visit went well."

"Yes. I talked to Scott Brenner this morning. Sara is behind that story in the *Herald*. Your guess was right, money."

"I said it!" Kenneth slapped his fist on the desk. "Why, though? I'm sure Anthony pays her adequately for her to want to do this."

"She also wants the girls, though Anthony says that's over his dead body. I just hope both of them can settle this amicably, so it doesn't become a protracted war. To me, she doesn't care if the case drags on till eternity."

"She's a mother. She should think about her children," Kenneth stated.

"Not many women do. Although I can understand some of her motivation. As a single mom, you want to have as many resources as you can because that added security is not there. It's not necessarily money-oriented, but you just think that additional money will solve the problem."

"That is still not an excuse."

"Which got me thinking, you know." She sat down. "Are you busy? I've had this idea brewing in my head, and I want to discuss it with you."

"I'll never be too busy for you, Nadia." Kenneth smiled, placing his arms on the desk. "What is it?"

"One of the papers I wrote at school was on the difficulties single mothers face especially in childcare."

When Emmett was two years old, Nadia started an online undergraduate psychology program, and later followed it up with a master's degree in early childhood education. Though she was running KNG Corporation, she had become fascinated with programs that progressed the causes of single mothers and the problems they faced on a day-to-day basis. While researching her paper, she surmised that if the problem of childcare was solved, a single mother had about fifty percent more chance of being as effective as a two-parent home. It had always been at the back of her mind to establish a holistic childcare center that catered to all facets of early childhood education and make it especially affordable for single mothers to keep their children in a safe and secure environment while they earned money for their families.

Kenneth listened intently as she talked. She had already made up her mind.

"How soon do you want to do this, Nadia? You know it's a big responsibility. Planning, city permits, Department of Family and Protective Services, location, etc. Don't you think it's going to be too much to bear at this time especially with you and Anthony just getting back together? He would want you to himself for a while you know."

"Trust me, I've thought about that." She laughed. "Maybe in the next two years. I'll see if I can get someone to have a plan ready by then."

"Yeah, it's actually a good idea," Kenneth said. "I'm really proud of you, girl. You know when Nick brought you home the first time, I was kind of hesitant. First, you were from Nigeria, and second, you were already pregnant with another man's child, though I didn't know the circumstances then. We had an awfully long talk after you left you know, but Mom and Aunt Lorraine were taken with you already and told us to just watch and see. I'm glad we took their advice. When I think of Nick…" His voice broke with emotion. "I'm just glad he was able to find happiness with you."

"Oh, Kenneth!" Nadia stood up to go give him a hug. "You guys are the best family ever. I couldn't have asked for more."

"Vera and I want you to be the godmother of our son."

"Wow…you're sure?" Nadia couldn't contain her excitement.

"Yes, she wouldn't have it any other way. Talking about that, her friends her throwing a surprise baby shower next week. I'll get the details and let you know. Will you be able to attend?"

Nadia laughed. "Do you need to even ask me that question? Try keeping me away!" She walked to the door. "Got to go now. I could stay here talking to you until tomorrow morning if I'm not careful."

"OK then. I'll be leaving in a couple minutes. See you later, Nadia."

Her Administrative Assistant was still at her desk, which surprised Nadia. Anything that kept Lisa on KNG Corporation premises until quarter till five must be really important. "You're still here?"

"Yes, Debbie needs these interview letters sent out, and her secretary called in sick today. So, I offered to help, but it was really busy, and I didn't get to them till well after four."

"Do you need help?"

"Oh no," Lisa said quickly. "I'm down to the last batch. I just need to put them in envelopes, and I'll be done. Some of the letters in your inbox need to be signed and sent out today, too."

"OK. Then, I'll get to them. They'll be ready to go in ten minutes."

"Yes, ma'am."

Indeed, there were more than letters waiting for Nadia in her office. Contracts that needed to be signed off on and emails that needed to be read and replied to. Only the security guard was in the lobby when she finally made her way out of the building at seven in the evening.

It was a cool evening, and the breeze blew lightly as she walked to her car, deep in thought. She looked around her, a safety measure Nick had taught her to observe when she worked at the gas station. Her car was in its usual place, but the car that was parked next to it was unfamiliar. Cautious, she didn't open her car, but reached slowly for her mace in her purse with her phone ready to go.

"Nadia, it's me," a voice said softly.

She gasped. It was Tunde, Kate's husband. "What are you doing here? Do you realize that I almost sprayed you?" She had only met him once at the hospital while visiting Anthony.

"Sorry. I had to come see you without getting noticed," he replied. He looked tired. "Do you have a minute?"

"Yes."

"Is everything OK?" The security guard had watched their exchange from the building entrance and came to see what was going on.

"It's OK, Tony. He's a friend. Thanks."

"Yes, ma'am." He turned around and left.

"I hope it's not serious," Nadia returned the mace to her bag. "Is everything OK?"

"It's not serious, just something I have to get off my chest. It's about you and Anthony."

"OK."

"And Kate."

Her body tensed then. "Please if you don't mind, I would prefer that you didn't discuss your wife with me."

"No, nothing of the sort. I just want to make things right between you and Anthony. The reason he abandoned you fifteen years ago is because Kate and Aunt Edna convinced him not to marry you."

Nadia couldn't even begin to comprehend where this was going. "What?"

"The day after you arrived in Houston, Anthony called his family from work. And they told him to send you away because you had gone behind their backs to get a US visa."

"Snuck behind them? How? That is ridiculous!" Nadia didn't know whether to laugh or cry. "I don't get. I was barely at their house and Kate and I didn't even talk. Besides, I stayed away from him after Aunt Edna went ballistic after seeing us together at his party. I find this really hard to believe."

"But it's the truth. According to Kate, both of you were discussing and figuring out ways to travel together. But you had gone behind her back, gotten your visa, and travelled without telling any of them, based on information that she gave you."

"My God." Nadia was speechless for a while. "How wicked can people be. So, they lied to Anthony about me out of jealousy, just because they had tried several times to travel and were denied visas, and Anthony sent me to live with strangers based on that. I blame him as much as I blame them. He should have known better."

"You have to consider his options, Nadia. He was trying to stay on his family's good side, so he listened to them. And you're not Igbo."

"Jesus! Don't go making any excuses for him, Tunde. What could they possibly have done to him from across the ocean? He didn't have to tell them anything about what was going on here!"

"True. But that is all in the past, Nadia. I know Anthony loves you very much because you are the only thing he talks about when I see him, and he can't wait to make it up to you. Especially as you have a son together. I want you all to be happy, OK?"

"All right. I really appreciate that you told me."

"No problem." He smiled. "I guess wedding bells will be ringing soon."

Nadia smiled but didn't say anything. "See you later."

That must be what Kate had been wanting to talk to her about, Nadia thought as she drove away. The fact that she gleaned this information from Tunde only made matters worse because she felt Anthony was still trying to cover up for Kate by not telling her the truth. Of course, he knew she would place some blame his way too for giving in to their conniving ways. The prospect of marrying him was not looking that good anymore as old memories and resentment started building back up again.

Anthony noticed the change immediately when he saw her two days later. He kept watching her closely and asking what was wrong, but she refused to tell him anything. She just sat at his bedside on a chair trying to be cheerful.

"Nadia, please tell me what's wrong?" he pleaded. "Is it something at the office?"

"Yes," she lied. "I'm trying to sort it out, though."

"You don't want to share? That may help, and I may have a solution for it?" he prompted.

She waved her hands. "Don't worry about me, Anthony. Do you feel you're ready to go home on Saturday?"

"I feel ready to go home now." He stood up from the bed and walked around the room. "Trying to get some light exercise in. You look so worried. I wish you'd tell me what's wrong so I can help."

"I'm good, Anthony." She stood up. "Got to go now" She headed for the door.

"No kiss?"

"OK." She walked back, gave him a light kiss on the lips, and left, leaving him watching her.

"Hi, Mom," Emmett greeted her at the door. "You're early today."

"Of course," Nadia sighed and placed her bag on a chair and sank into the welcoming softness of the couch. "It was a rough day at work. Two employees from the IT department resigned today. They both got new jobs in Dubai. Can you believe that? Now we have to start looking for two people who can fill their shoes. They were good employees, too."

"Senora, you want something to drink?" said Roberta, coming from the kitchen with a big smile as usual. "I make strawberry sangria. You want some?"

"Si, Roberta, pequenos." Nadia had grown to like the beverage made from strawberries, white wine, orange, and sparkling water. "You have food?"

"Me always have food, senora. Tortillas, chicken quesadillas, paella, chili con queso y tacos—"

"OK. OK, Roberta. Paella, si!" Nadia laughed.

"Un momento, por favor! I bring food." The nanny left.

"Is everything all right, Mom?" Emmett asked when Roberta left. "You've been kind of distracted lately."

"Nothing you need worry about," Nadia dismissed lightly. There was no point bothering Emmett with grownup business. He had been through enough as it was. She shifted the focus to him. "You ready to go back to school next week?"

"I can't wait, Mom, though I won't be doing sports right away. Probably in a couple of months. The coach called me today."

"Aww, that's so nice of him. I'm sure your teammates can't wait to have you back in their midst, wreaking havoc on unsuspecting teams."

"You make it sound like we are going to war," Emmett joked.

"Food ready!" Roberta yelled as she placed dishes on the table.

"Have you eaten?"

"More than enough." Emmett followed her to the dining table, pulling out a chair first for his mom before sitting down. "Are you and Dad going to get married as soon as he's back?"

"Who gave you that idea?"

He shrugged. "I just thought…"

"We are working on it. Hmm…yummy. I might just take Roberta home with me when everything settles. This is better than eating at a restaurant," Nadia said.

"Mom, you're avoiding my question."

"Emmett, you know marriage is a serious issue, not something to go into lightly."

"But he loves you," he argued.

"Love and marriage are two different things. Not that I should be discussing any of this with you. Now go get some exercise and leave me to eat in peace."

"Are we going back home after Dad comes back?"

"What do you want to do?" Nadia's voice softened. She could feel the turmoil in Emmett's demeanor. She really didn't want him to feel that he would have to choose between his parents.

"I'm coming home with you, of course. But I'll be visiting him, too. At least until y'all get married."

"There you go again with that marriage thing. Go play a game or watch TV or something, Emmett."

Morayode

Anthony was in high spirits when his father picked him up on Saturday, accompanied by the nurse. After strict instructions from Dr. Livingston on how to manage his health, they said their goodbyes to all the hospital staff who had been taking care of him and left. Though he protested, the hospital insisted that he had to have a wheelchair until he was in the car taking him home.

The nurse drove, Emmett beside her, and Nadia was with Anthony in the back. He held on to her hand as soon as they entered the car. They couldn't talk much, but she could see the relief on his face.

"It's good to be out of the hospital," he said.

"I know. You have to take it easy though for a while, nothing strenuous. You heard the doctor. Don't get home and start thinking you're Superman."

"I'm just grateful to be alive. Can we stop at Jack in the Box? I need to get my hands on a sourdough grilled chicken club!"

"Wow! You're hungry!" Nadia joked. "Stop at Jack in the Box. Drive-thru," she directed to the nurse.

"I called Sara today to see if she can bring the girls by tomorrow. I've missed them."

"I'm sure they miss you, too."

"Will you be there?"

"I'm not sure yet. I have to go home and check on things in the morning."

They soon found a Jack in the Box and ordered some food. The rest of the drive home was quiet.

"Is Roberta not here?" Anthony asked as the nurse parked the car. The house was in darkness except for a light in the backyard.

"She was here when we left, and I told her not to go anywhere," Nadia said, winking at Emmett.

"Hmm…" They left the car with Nadia in front, and the rest behind them. When they got to the door, she turned to Anthony. "Will you do the honors?"

He rang the doorbell. Roberta opened the door.

"Why are the lights off Roberta?" Anthony demanded. "Did something happen?"

"Senor, welcome!" Roberta shouted with joy. "You back home. Muy bueno!"

Just then, the lights turned on with lots of cheers from well-wishers, friends, and family who had come to welcome Anthony home. He saw familiar faces filled with love and care, and emotions welled up inside him.

He stood at the threshold, at a loss for words as Nadia held his hand. A tear escaped his eye.

CHAPTER TEN

The last guest left at eleven thirty. Despite the short time it took to gather people together, it was a successful celebration, nonetheless.

Anthony lay on the couch, exhausted, his head resting on Nadia's lap. Emmett had gone to bed earlier, tired and worn out after all the preparation into getting the party ready.

"You shouldn't have gone to all the trouble, and I didn't know so many people cared."

"Of course, they care. We are blessed with good friends," Nadia said. "Everything was last-minute, and they still showed up. I was surprised David and Scott brought their wives, too."

"So was I. Thanks, Nadia. I owe you a lot already." He sat up and sat close to her. Nadia didn't resist when he pulled her into his arms. "Just know that I appreciate all you've done in the past three months: the support, the hospital visits, staying on top of my treatment with Dr. Livingston. I couldn't ask for more. I am so glad this happened with you and not Sara."

"Don't say such a thing, Anthony. If you were still married to her, of course, she would do the same." She felt so secure and safe in the comfort of his strong arms.

"So why was she not here tonight? She could, at least, have shown up even if for a few minutes."

"Leave that alone, Anthony. Unless you still care for her, let it go."

"I need to get the girls back as soon as I can."

"Get better first."

"So, what's going to happen now? You're going back to your place as soon as I'm better?"

"The future will decide. We're not married yet, and I can't just leave my house sitting empty."

"I have a feeling you're stalling."

"Why would you think that?" Nadia said defensively.

He shrugged. "Just a feeling. I'm so tired now." He stood up. "Can't wait to sleep in my bed for once."

"Yes, let me take you upstairs. I need a shower badly myself." Nadia waited in his room as he got ready for bed wanting to make sure he was OK. "Are you all right?"

"Yes,"

"Good. Then, I'll see you in the morning," Nadia said.

He stood in his robe in the middle of the room, staring at her. "Where are you going?"

"To my room, of course. I've told you nothing until after marriage. Good thing you have so many rooms in here."

"I want you to stay."

"No." She gave him a light kiss.

"Nadia, why are you being so difficult? I haven't had time to hold you since forever, and you're going to sleep in a separate room my first night back home?"

"I don't want history repeating itself."

"That's the most ridiculous thing I ever heard. What could I possibly do to you in this state of weakness?" He was getting angrier by the minute. "So, all this you've been doing is for show?"

"How dare you—" Nadia's arm was stopped by his hand as he drew her to him.

"Remember the last time you did that? I told you never ever to raise your hands to me ever again."

"Let me go, Anthony!" she whispered.

"Not yet, I think all this fierceness is because no man has warmed your bed in a while." He claimed her lips in a deep and searing kiss as he held her tightly. "God, I needed that, even if you didn't!" He pushed her away gently. He was breathing heavily. It was obvious he was as affected by the kiss as she was. "Go to your room if you want to, Nadia. There's plenty of time."

She left without a word. Nadia was peeved by his words even if what he said was true. It had been a while and she had been feeling the loneliness more the past few months. With Anthony's reappearance, it had dissipated a little but she felt something was still missing. She wanted the warmth and authenticity she had with Nick because she never had to doubt his love for her. Anthony had betrayed her many times and still doing so by not telling her the real reason behind his behavior years back.

Kate had been at the party too with her husband, but apart from a brief "hi", she went out of her way to avoid her until they left. She just couldn't understand where the hatred was from. Okafors were certainly not better than her family growing up, although they had more privileges mostly because they had relatives who lived abroad and helped them out. Nadia wondered if she would know any peace if she married Anthony. If he didn't make her life miserable, his family certainly would. She was having none of that foolishness for herself or Emmett.

"Rise and shine, Mom!" Emmett was in her room the next morning with a breakfast tray he placed on a side desk.

"Emmett, what time is it?" Nadia burrowed her head into the pillows, not ready to get up yet. "It's Sunday for God's sake, Emmett!"

"Dad and I made breakfast. He gave Roberta the day off, too," Emmett said. "English muffins, eggs, bacon, and your coffee just the way you like it, with lots of cream."

"Your dad is up already?" Nadia sat up, still groggy. "He's forgotten what the doctor said?"

"It's ten o'clock, Mom,"

"Hmm...I've got to go brush. I hope the food tastes as good as it smells."

"Of course, Mom, what do you think?" Emmett joked and left the room.

The food did taste good. Nadia ate every last crumb and got dressed in slate gray clam diggers and white T-shirt before taking the tray back downstairs. She could hear Anthony and Emmett in the living room, discussing the news as they watched TV. Emmett's voice was starting to break even and sounded more and more like Anthony's every day.

"Thanks for the breakfast," she said as she sat next to Emmett on the couch. Anthony was on the recliner. "I hope you guys have eaten, though."

Anthony looked at her narrowly, as if weighing her mood from their conversation the night before. "I called Sara and she said she couldn't bring the girls. Do you mind picking them up for me?"

"Anthony, I really don't want to start getting in between you and your ex-wife."

"Got to go," Emmett hastily excused himself. "Got to call my friends." He put a hand to his ear.

"That boy," Anthony laughed. "He sure knows when to take his leave."

"We could go together," he suggested. "You'll drive, of course. I really want to see them."

Nadia contemplated for a few minutes. "OK."

"Thanks, Nadia," Anthony said quietly. "Emmett can come along with us if he wants."

It turned out to be a very good day. After picking up the girls they visited the park for an impromptu picnic, so Anthony could get some fresh air. Nadia was glad to see the girls and Emmett getting along so well, but Anthony was broody. He would talk for some time then become silent.

"Are you OK? I hope you took your meds this morning."

He had been placed on several immunosuppressant medications for the rest of his life to prevent present and future organ rejection by his body.

"I'm OK," he said reflectively. "Just thinking about the vanity of life. What would I have done if not for our son?"

"God would still have sent someone else I believe."

"You go through that and come out knowing how much the little things count. I want us to be a happy family, Nadia, but I know you're stalling, and I wonder why."

"Give me time, Anthony."

"Don't you love me?"

"I do," Nadia replied. "I just want to be sure."

"About what? I know there's nothing that I could give you that you don't already have, except love."

"Give me time," she said simply.

"All right. All right. Can I get a kiss, though?" He was on a reclining picnic chair.

"In front of the kids?" She bent over him and gave him a kiss anyway.

The three of them soon settled into a somewhat routine "family" life. Nadia could see that it made Emmett happy to see them together. Anthony was not the best of patients for a while, and they had to change nurses after only two weeks of him being back home. He hated not being at the office though David and Scott Brenner brought work to him at home sometimes.

Nadia could see the frustration on his face and alleviated his misery by accompanying him on long walks to regain his strength. The walks were mostly pleasant, and sometimes they came back home all mad at each other over the littlest thing.

One thing she really enjoyed was having Erin and Yazmine over at the house. The girls were always a breath of fresh air. Once, they came into her room, smiling mischievously. Nadia looked from one to the other in curiosity.

"Are you going to marry our dad?" Yazmine blurted.

"Girls!" Nadia chided playfully. "Now, now, that is not something you should worry about."

"But we want you to," Erin said. "He loves you."

"Really? And what do you girls know about love?"

They both jumped onto her bed without a care. "We know it makes you feel like you have butterflies in your belly," Erin explained.

"Oh no," Nadia put her hand to her chest and proceeded to tell the girls a little bit about the birds and the bees. "Let me tell you something, girls, all you need to do now is focus on your education. If any boy comes along and tells you he loves you, ask him to cut his heart out and give it to you, and see how fast he runs."

The girls laughed.

"I'm serious, girls. Anyway, leave your father and me to sort ourselves out, OK?" Nadia advised. "Let's go get some ice cream and see if there's anything good on TV."

Nadia was having a restless night. She tossed and turned on the bed as a bad dream threatened to take her down the abyss.

"Nick!" she screamed, breaking out in cold sweat as reality hit her. She sat up abruptly, shocked to find Anthony seated by her side, watching in silence. "What are you doing here?" she whispered.

"You were having a bad dream, and you called out Nick's name," he said softly.

She looked away from him, feeling naked in front of his eyes. "That still doesn't explain why you're here."

"Nadia, do you know how many times I've sat here and watched you sleep? And do you know how many times you've called out Nick's name in your dreams?"

"Really?"

"Yes, really." He nodded. "I've known for a while why you're hesitant to marry me, and I do respect that you need time, but you seriously need to see a doctor or something."

"Are you suggesting I see a psychiatrist?"

"I don't know. Nick has been dead for fifteen years, and you still dream about him and call out his name. I don't think that's normal."

"I know…I feel like I want to let go but a part of me just won't. He was a very important part of my life."

"You have to let go, Nadia. In fact, you have to sort out a lot of things, including your feelings for me. I definitely wouldn't want us to get married with you still carrying the torch for a dead man."

"You make it really ugly when you say it that way, Anthony. I do love you."

"Hmm…in a way I envy the love you have for him."

"Oh Anthony." She held his hands. "You don't need to do that. I do love you."

"You sure have a strange way of showing it, though. I know something is eating at you and you refuse to tell me."

"I need a man who's going to be honest with me and make me feel safe. I don't want a relationship where I have to second-guess everything you tell me."

"Why would I lie to you or otherwise? I have been nothing but open and honest with you."

"Because you've done it and are still doing it."

Anthony was puzzled. "There's obviously something you're not telling me."

"Yes. Why did you abandon me fifteen years ago with not as much as a goodbye? How did you think I felt being pregnant with no one to turn to? And believe me, I'm not mad at you. I just want to know the truth."

"There's no truth to tell, Nadia, I've apologized to you so many times already. It shouldn't be that hard to make up your mind if you really love me. Stop giving excuses, 'cos I'm getting tired of them." He stood up abruptly and left the room.

"Anthony!"

He didn't look back.

Nadia checked her cell phone. It was just two in the morning. She pulled the coverlet over her and tried to force herself to sleep.

The next day, Emmett entered her room as she was packing.

"We're leaving, Mom?"

"Yes, go pack your stuff."

"Why?"

"It's time, Emmett. We can't just abandon our house and live here indefinitely OK."

"But Mom—"

"Look, young man, go pack your things and that's that!" she yelled. "It's time to go!"

Emmett hesitated only a moment before he shrugged and obeyed her instructions. She didn't say goodbye to Anthony before she left and waited for Emmett in the car.

He was sulky when he came back and wouldn't talk to her. She dropped him off at school and drove home. She went in late to work, was distracted, and left early. Absentmindedly, she drove through traffic, and only realized she had gone to Anthony's house after parking the car. Furious at herself, she started the car back up and drove home.

The house that used to be welcoming didn't seem as inviting as she let herself in. Her demeanor at work had given Kenneth some concern, but he didn't press her into telling him anything. She had snapped at poor Lisa for the first time ever and had to reschedule several meetings in order to combat a sudden onset of migraine, but her head pounded not with a physical headache but the mental anguish of unresolved issues and long-held emotions. Was Anthony right that she was still holding on to Nick though he was long gone? Was that the reason she'd never established any permanent relationship in fifteen years? She definitely had the offers and chances but always held back for some unidentifiable reason.

She managed to cook dinner, a light affair of baked chicken with coconut rice and mixed vegetables on the side. Emmett was more cheerful when he came back from school, but he spent the entire evening in his room instead of sitting and talking like they usually did in the dining or living room after dinner. She left him alone. He might think her unreasonable, but he would appreciate her hesitation with time.

Anthony didn't call. She called his phone twice. When he didn't pick up, she called Roberta, who answered her phone and assured her that "Senor is fine, resting."

The next day was much better at work, and Nadia came in late but was surprised that Emmett was not yet back at seven. She didn't call him right away because practice sometimes went on till eight in the night. She called his phone at eight fifteen.

"Emmett, where are you?" she demanded, relief setting in. "I was beginning to get worried."

"I'm with Dad," he replied simply.

"Why didn't you tell me you'd be going over there?"

"Sorry, Mom, I didn't want to upset you."

"Is your dad there?"

"Yes,"

"Let me talk to him."

"You should have called me, Anthony," she voiced quietly. Now wasn't the time to get mad. She felt the pain that Emmett had to start deciding some things on his own and might sometimes not pick her in favor of his dad, but she wouldn't hold it against him, either.

"I was asleep when he got here, Nadia. I was just about to call you in fact. He's in good hands. Don't worry about him, OK?"

"OK. Can I talk to him again?"

"Sure."

Emmett was apologetic as he talked to her. "I had to come make sure he's OK, Mom. I hope you don't mind. I'll let you know next time."

"When are you coming back home?"

"Tomorrow, after school."

"All right."

"Good night. I love you, Mom."

"I love you too, son."

But Nadia knew something had changed in their relationship. She would have to tread carefully so as not to drive a wedge between them where Anthony was concerned. The emptiness of the house loomed more than ever. She missed Emmett. And if she would admit it to herself, she missed Anthony, too.

When Anthony's call came in during her take-away lunch in the office she picked it up immediately.

"Nadia."

"Yes."

"Sorry about yesterday, I didn't even know he was coming over," Anthony started.

"It's OK. He's your son, and right now we can't force him to choose between us."

"That's right, but I've told him he should let you know before doing something like that again. My parents are coming from Nigeria next week. They're visiting for a month or so."

"Wow! That's good! I'll come by and see them sometime."

"Yes, all right, Nadia. Talk later, OK?"

"Bye." She hung up.

Kenneth walked into the room. "Anthony?"

"Yes."

"You're really giving that man a hard time," he mentioned.

"He said I need to see a psychiatrist," Nadia said.

"Why on Earth?"

"He thinks I'm still hung up on Nick."

"That might not be too far from the truth."

Nadia looked up at him. "You too?"

"I haven't seen you with any man in fifteen years. That's a very long time, and you are still young," Kenneth said. "Any doctor will tell you that's not healthy at all."

"Is it not just about sex?"

"You know it's not that simple. I don't want to start sounding like one of your girlfriends but companionship, a shoulder to cry on sometimes, and all of the above including what you just mentioned."

"You're incorrigible, Kenneth," Nadia laughed. "But don't worry I'll sort myself out with time."

"Hope so,"

"How are Vera and the baby?"

"Good, I'm totally out of the picture for now. That baby is the only person she sees, and I can't even afford to be jealous when I see them together. She's happy. I'm happy."

"She'll come around, Kenneth, give her time. I hope you're changing diapers, though.

"What do you think? We even take turns waking up at night to feed the baby. It's not easy at all I'm even scared to have a second child now," Kenneth said. "If they take so much of your time when they're little what can you expect when they grow up? And everybody keeps telling me I ain't seen nothing yet." He made air quotes with his fingers. "Wait for the terrible twos!"

"Oh my God, don't tell me you're tired already?" Nadia laughed. "You have eighteen years to go in case you don't know."

"Bring it on!" Kenneth beat his chest playfully. "I'm just kidding, Nadia. I love that baby to death, but it's still hard work. Now I know why you feel the way you do about single mothers. Or even single fathers as a matter of fact. Raising a child is not a joke."

The receptionist came in to announce that Anthony was waiting to see her. Nadia was surprised, but also glad that his apologies about barging into her office were not in vain. He walked in into the office as she and Kenneth laughed together.

"How are you feeling man?" said Kenneth.

"Much better, Kenneth, thank you. Do you mind if I have a moment alone with, Nadia?"

"Not at all." Kenneth gave a quick wink and left.

Nadia sighed. "You should be resting, Anthony. What is so urgent that you couldn't call or wait till later? Besides, I talked to you earlier." She couldn't help but notice his leaner frame underneath the chinos and polo shirt.

"I've come to take you out to lunch."

"I had lunch already."

He sat down anyway. "You very busy?"

"Not really. This is still my office, though. You know I don't like you coming in here, unannounced, like you own the company? What do you want my staff to think?" This was said lightly though, with a smile.

"I believe you hire the smartest and the brightest, Nadia. If they haven't figured out yet that we're together, then something is definitely wrong," he quipped.

She looked at him coolly. "So why are you here?"

"Needed to see you. I'm going crazy in that house by myself. And I swear Roberta is trying to feed me to death."

That elicited a laugh from her. "I bet!"

"I miss you, Nadia, I want you to come back. Stay in your room, whatever. I just want to know you're around. And Sara and I have come to an agreement. She agrees to the initial arrangement if I raise her monthly allowance a few thousand dollars, which is OK by me. I want you around when the girls come back."

"What would the children think? We're not married and—"

"Nadia." He stood up, came to stand by her, and drew her up to him. "Marry me."

"Not yet." She evaded his kiss. "Once you get better."

"We both know that's an excuse. I know we don't want anything elaborate. We can just go downtown and get it over with," he said. "And I think I know why you've been stalling."

"Really, you finally figured it out?"

"Yes, you're still mad at me for—"

He was cut short by the phone on Nadia's desk. She picked it up. "Lisa...oh, yes, I almost forgot." She turned to Anthony. "I have a department head meeting in five minutes, Anthony. I'll come by later after work."

"Think about it, OK?" he said before he left.

The longing in his eyes tugged at her heart. She almost ran into his arms then but steeled herself. "I'll come see you after work."

The meeting lasted longer than usual. Nadia got several text messages on her phone that she had a visitor in the office, but Lisa wouldn't say who it was. When she finally found out it was Kate, it was with a mixture of curiosity and cautiousness that she ushered her into the office.

"Hi."

"Hi, Nadia. I was hoping we could talk."

"OK." She already knew the reason why. "I hope it's not serious."

"Not at all. I've come to ask for your forgiveness."

"I thought we took care of that at the hospital, Kate. The past is past. Let's move on with life in the present."

"No, I must tell you this. I am the reason Anthony kicked you out of his house when you came to Houston."

Nadia let it soak in, then looked at Kate for a long time. "You know, we are both women, and we were both girls once. I just couldn't understand what I've done to deserve the kind of treatment you dish out to me. You were older than me. So why the hatred?"

Kate shrugged. "I can't explain it myself. You were such a smart girl, and even though your father was strict you seemed to know what you wanted even in secondary school. You didn't care what anybody thought, and you were you. I guess I envied that. I became even more jealous when I read your stories in the newspapers in Nigeria back then. To me you were living a glamorous life, going to all these events and talking to all these sports celebrities."

"Trust me, it wasn't what you thought at all. Do you know how many miles a poor freelance journalist has to walk before she gets even a decent story that will be paid for by newspapers? And having to deal with a father that is constantly looking over your shoulder? I thought you guys were the lucky ones, going to church in your fancy dresses every Sunday and riding around in cars sent by relatives from abroad."

"What fools we were," Kate said. "I can't believe I was that spoiled."

"Hmm…" Nadia left that alone.

"And then Anthony had written so many letters of invitation to the US Embassy, but they kept refusing me a visa. So, when I heard that you traveled, I was mad. And I knew that Anthony liked you because I could see the way he paid special attention to you at the party. When he called and said you were staying with him, I was so jealous, so I told him that you had used information I gave you to get your visa even though both of us were processing it together. And my mom and Aunt Edna kind of went along with it because they were afraid that if you stayed with him, he might marry you. We also told him he couldn't marry an outsider, somebody from a different tribe."

"Well." was all Nadia could say. Many marriages in Nigeria were prevented from happening because of tribal differences, something Nadia didn't understand. It wasn't like the family was going to live with the couple, yet in these modern times such thinking was still an issue. Somehow, though, she felt relief at hearing it from the horse's mouth, although that still didn't exonerate Anthony for listening to some women before taking that costly decision to send her out of his house the next day.

"It's all right, Kate. Destiny will be no matter how human beings try to manipulate life."

"I know better now," Kate agreed. "I mean Emmett is really destiny's child. Despite all our lies and conniving ways, see how he ends up saving Anthony's life. Aunt Edna actually told me to apologize to you after your visit to Nigeria, but I just couldn't get myself to. And now Mom is insisting that she must see you when she and Dad are here. I don't know if Anthony has told you, but they're coming to the US for a visit."

"Yes, he told me."

"So, you forgive him?"

"Anthony has a mind of his own," Nadia said simply.

"True, but please just find it in your heart. He really loves you. And if he's not telling you why it's because he's trying to protect me. He's just wired that way, so he takes the blame for himself."

"It's all right, Kate. Thanks for coming by, I really appreciate it." Nadia walked around her desk to give the other woman a hug. "All is well."

"Thanks."

"Kate, can I say something before you leave?" Nadia said hesitantly.

"Anything, Nadia."

"It's about you and Tunde. He is a good man Kate. I know it's not in my place to say, but you need to make your home a happy one especially for the kids."

"Thanks, Nadia." They both hugged, and Nadia, even though she hadn't done anything wrong, felt as if a heavy weight had been lifted off her shoulders. She couldn't wait to see Anthony.

Surely, that was the longest drive she'd ever taken, Nadia thought as she pulled up in Anthony's driveway later. She had gone home to shower and change and also check on Emmett before heading over there. Her nerves were in high gear, and she stayed in the car several minutes before finally stepping out to ring the doorbell. She expected Roberta, but he opened the door promptly, dressed in casual shorts and shirt. She hadn't noticed it when he was in her office earlier, but he had a stubble which made him look even sexier as he stood at the doorway taking in her appearance. He seemed to approve the casual but chic simple chambray knee-length T-shirt dress and booties.

"Nadia."

"Hi, Anthony. Can we talk here, or would you prefer we go somewhere?"

"Let's do it here, Nadia. I think I overextended myself today, and I'm feeling a little bit tired." He waved her into the house. "You look really nice."

"Thanks." She sat on the couch.

"I gave Roberta the evening off. You want something to drink?"

"You don't happen to have some of that strawberry sangria, do you?"

"Yeah, yeah, I think she makes it and stores in the fridge just for you." He went into the kitchen, but she followed him.

"I can get it myself."

"Go sit, Nadia. I'm not helpless."

"And I'm not a stranger here," she protested as she got a glass and set it on the table while Anthony retrieved a pitcher from the fridge. He poured some into her glass, and they went back to the living room. "I had a visitor at the office today."

"Who?"

"Take a guess."

He shook his head. "I can't. Is it somebody I know?"

"Yes," Nadia said. "Kate, your sister."

"Why? I hope she didn't start a fight right there."

"Why would you think that?"

"Because she's my sister, and I know her. And everybody knows you guys don't like each other. Correction, everybody knows she doesn't like you for whatever reason."

"Don't talk about your sister like that."

"Hmm…I love her, but she's no saint." Anthony left the recliner to come sit by her on the couch. He was so close she could see the pulse in his neck. "So, what did she say?"

Nadia shook her head, looking at him with love and tenderness. "You're a fool, Anthony," she said softly. "If she didn't spill the beans about what happened fifteen years ago, were you ever going to tell me? You never figured out why I was being cautious with you?"

"I'm a man, Nadia. We are supposed to protect those we love. Even if Kate didn't tell you, I would have found a way to tell you later maybe not in so many words."

"So, you were willing to suffer in misery? But you are not totally excused, though. You knew what you were doing. How could you just let me go like that if you really loved me?"

"Look at it this way, Nadia. Things happen for a reason. What if I'd not given in to their demand to send you out of my house, and they'd discovered that you were pregnant, and pressured me into making you get rid of the baby? And if I'd married you, they would have made life hell for you. You wouldn't have been happy in the marriage and we would have ended up divorced."

"You would never do such a thing, Anthony!" she exclaimed. "Or would you? Pressuring me to get rid of the baby?"

"As I sit here beside you today, let me tell you that I would have been overjoyed for you to be pregnant with my child. But back then, who knows? I am being totally honest with you. Anything could have happened. One thing I knew back then, and I am even surer of now, is my love for you. I had to force myself to love Sara, but the love I have for you came freely and will always be."

"Oh, Anthony...I do love you too, very much," she whispered.

"Come here, Nadia, baby girl." He kissed her long and hard. They nestled together on the couch, one heart beating as one. "Does that mean you're staying with me tonight?" He smiled as he caressed her cheek.

"No, Emmett is home by himself, so I have to go. You could come with me though you'll be staying in a separate room."

"I'm not even going to complain." Anthony laughed as they left the house. "I love you, Nadia."

"Likewise."

"Likewise? What's that supposed to mean?"

"OK, I love you, too. Plenty millions."

"That's much better" he gave her a tender kiss on the cheek. "A million times better."

www.ingramcontent.com/pod-product-compliance
Lightning Source LLC
Chambersburg PA
CBHW060135130626
46556CB00006B/2352